The Struggle

Striving to Survive

The Struggle

Striving to Survive

Johnny Franklin Jr.

ELITE PUBLISHING PRESS

The Struggle: Striving to Survive

Copyright © 2021 by Johnny Franklin Jr.

johnny.lee.franklin@gmail.com

Elite Publishing Press

Library of Congress Cataloging-in-Publication Data is available upon request.

ISBN 978-1-7336321-3-3 (Paperback)

ISBN 978-1-7336321-4-0 (Ebook)

ISBN 978-1-7336321-5-7 (Hardcover)

Cover design by Johnny Franklin Jr.

Printed in the United States of America

In the ghetto, the struggle is real.

Chapter One

IT WAS ANOTHER ordinary morning in the ghetto. The neighborhood dogs are outside barking non-stop and the sunlight is slightly coming through my window blinds. While pulling the covers from over my head, I see my little brother Cameron sound asleep on the other side of my room. Apparently, he spent the whole night playing my video game again and forgot he has a room of his own down the hall.

"Wake up bro!" I yell, while wiping the crust out of my eyes. "Get up and get out my room. I need my privacy now."

Cameron starts slowly waking up, stretching his arms wide and yawning.

"Did you get enough beauty rest?" I ask. "I see you spent the whole night on the video game again."

"Yeah, you know it!" Cameron says. "I was up playing for a long time and just went to sleep right here when I got tired."

My little brother Cameron is a game fanatic. He can sit in front of the television and play video games for hours. I can relate to how much he enjoys playing video games because I used to be the same way when I was his age.

"I'm glad you had fun last night bro," I say. "But I need my privacy right now if you don't mind."

"Okay bro," Cameron says, as he stands up from the bean bag chair he fell asleep in.

That old chair has really had its days and will be heading to the trash soon. Mama gave it to me years ago and I just passed it on down to Cameron. I don't see how he slept in it because that old thing is really worn out.

"I'm going to the kitchen in a minute," Cameron says. "I need to see if Mama is cooking because I'm hungry."

"Okay," I say. "Do your thing little man."

"Don't forget to go brush your teeth after you have your privacy."

I toss one of my pillows at Cameron on his way out of my room, but he closes the door before I can hit him. He can be somewhat annoying at times, but I love my little brother with all my heart. He really looks up to me and follows me around whenever the opportunity presents itself.

As I roll out of bed and look around for some socks, I hear noises coming from the front of the house. As Cameron mentioned, Mama is probably in the kitchen making breakfast while listening to the radio.

As I leave my room and head toward the kitchen, Cameron flies right past me in a hurry. He bumps me as he passes by and nearly knocks me down.

"*Slow down there boy*," I say.

"I have to get to the kitchen before you eat up everything," Cameron says. "We all know how you get down in this house."

As I make my way down the hall and walk into the kitchen, Cameron has already grabbed a plate from the dish drain and is standing in front of the stove. Mama has the refrigerator open, taking out a jug of orange juice.

"Good morning Mama," I say.

"Morning handsome," Mama says. "Breakfast is ready, so you boys can just dig in."

My beautiful mama, Sophia Johnson, is the strongest and hardest working woman I know. She looks very tired this morning. As usual, she has her hair pulled back in a ponytail. She probably just got in from working a double shift because she's still wearing her work uniform. I really hate that Mama has to work so hard to take care of Cameron and I by herself. I know it's not easy for her one bit. She's the only person Cameron and I can rely on. With me being the oldest, I'm considered as the man of the house.

"So, did you boys sleep good last night?" Mama asks.

"I slept alright Mama," Cameron says, as he sits down at the kitchen table.

"What about you Avery?" Mama asks.

"I slept good," I say. "I woke up to Cameron asleep in my room again. He got a video game in his room, but he just chooses to come in my room when I'm asleep and play my game."

"Cameron, why were you in Avery's room?" Mama asks.

"I was *scared* last night," Cameron says. "When I was in my room playing my game, I heard people arguing and gun shots outside. I went to Avery's room, but I didn't wake him up so he wouldn't get mad at me."

"I'm so tired of this crazy neighborhood," Mama says. "There are gun shots going off just about every other night. If I could, I'd move us out of this place. I'm sorry you had to deal with that last night baby boy. You should've gotten your brother up."

"Cameron, I wouldn't have gotten mad if you woke me up," I say.

"That's not true," he says.

"I promise I wouldn't have gotten mad at you little bro."

"Whatever. You always get mad when somebody wake you up from a deep sleep."

"He's not lying," Mama says. "You can be very grouchy when somebody wake you up from a deep sleep. You be ready to fight."

"I do not be like that," I say.

"Avery, stop all that lying boy," Mama says.

"When are we going to move Mama?" Cameron asks. "I get tired of hearing the gun shots all the time."

"I don't know baby boy," Mama says, as she pours herself a glass of orange juice. "When I get a better job and save up some money, I can get us somewhere else to stay. Until then, we'll be right here."

"What about when you get your taxes next year Mama?" Cameron asks.

"I got this boy," Mama says. "I don't need your help when it comes to making money decisions. Stay in your place. You just focus on staying out of trouble."

After making my plate and setting it on the table, I head over to the refrigerator to get some milk. When I open the refrigerator, there's no milk inside. As a matter of fact, the refrigerator is nearly empty. The only thing we have left in the refrigerator is a jug of Kool-Aid that Mama made a few days ago and a bottle of ketchup on the bottom rack.

"Mama, we're out of milk," I say.

"I know son," Mama says. "I didn't have enough money to get some milk from the store yesterday. I'll be going back to the store in a few days."

Cameron frowns and says, "That means I won't be able to eat my cereal today."

"Don't worry little bro," I say. "I'll go get some milk from the store later today."

"Cool," Cameron says.

Since we don't have any milk, orange juice will be my selection this morning. I'm not drinking Kool-Aid with my breakfast today. I sit down at the table and begin to eat my food.

When Cameron finishes eating, he puts his plate into the sink and runs off to his room. Now that he's finally gone, I can have a real talk with Mama.

"Is everything alright Mama?" I ask.

"We're in pretty bad shape at the moment," she says. "We'll still make it like we always do. Don't worry."

"This is the first time I've ever seen the refrigerator like that," I say. "We don't have *anything* in there."

"I know son," she says with a sad look on her face. "Money is kind of short right now, but I'll figure something out eventually."

"Do I need to get a job to help out around the house Mama?" I ask.

"No. You just need to concentrate on staying out of trouble and keeping your grades up when school starts. You'll be going back in two weeks."

"I never get into trouble Mama and I promise to keep my grades up. With this being my senior year and all, I really have to be on top of everything. I want to go to college."

"That's what I like to hear son. You can do whatever you put your mind to. Going to college will help you get out of this awful neighborhood and make something of yourself. I believe in you."

"Thanks for believing in me."

"You know I always got your back son."

"I know. How is your job going Mama?"

"It's going alright. It's been helping us maintain and keep a roof over our heads, but I do need another job that pays more. I've been looking around recently, but I haven't been able to find anything yet."

Mama has been working at a warehouse for a few months now. The way things are currently going, we'll never have enough food in the refrigerator unless she finds a better paying job.

"This warehouse job may not last too much longer either," she says. "They're already talking about cutting hours and laying off a few people soon. I'll be at the library this weekend doing more job applications online. I hope I can find something quick."

"If you ever need my help, just say the word Mama," I say. "I can always pick up a little part-time job while I'm in school."

"You don't have to do that," she says. "Just do what I already told you to do. I got everything under control. What are you doing with yourself today?"

"I'll be hanging out with Derek," I say. "I'm stopping by his house on my way to the store later today."

"Tell that boy I said hello," she says.

"Will do Mama. Get yourself some rest after you finish eating your food. You look extremely tired."

"I will son. They worked us hard last night. My feet are kind of sore."

I get up from the kitchen table, place my dishes into the sink, and head to my room.

When I walk into my room, Cameron is sitting on my bed with his arms folded. Little man just cannot stay out of my room.

"What do you want little bro?" I ask.

"I'm not stupid you know," Cameron says. "I know there's something wrong."

"You're talking crazy," I say. "Everything is cool."

"I was listening when you and Mama were talking in the kitchen," he says. "What are we going to do?"

This boy is always eavesdropping on people private conversations.

"I guarantee that we'll be just fine Cameron," I say. "Mama will get a better job soon or later and then we'll be good."

"But what if she can't get a better job?"

"She will. You don't have to worry about that. We're good bro."

Cameron smiles and says, "Okay. I trust you big bro."

The last thing I want is my little brother to worry about us being able to survive. Worrying about surviving shouldn't be on an eight-year-old's brain at all. If Mama doesn't find a better job soon, I really don't know what we're going to do. We can't make it with an empty refrigerator.

Cameron finally leaves my room for good. I'll check on him a little later. Now, I can take a quick shower, throw on some clothes, and hit the streets. I hope today will be a good day.

Chapter Two

ONCE I MAKE my way out of the house, Derek's house is my next destination. Derek has been my best friend since middle school. He lives just a couple blocks over from my house. Derek has always had my back when I've needed help. We have a very strong bond and I consider Derek as family. As I walk to Derek's house, the hot sun is beaming down on my head. It feels like 98 degrees outside. The summer is slowly coming to an end and I surely won't miss these scorching hot days. I'm sure the neighborhood junkies won't miss these scorching hot days either. Right now, there's plenty of them walking up and down the street. I bet most of them are searching for their next opportunity to get high. As I approach Derek's house, he's outside sitting on the porch.

"What's up bro?" Derek yells.

"Nothing much," I say. "I've just been at the house taking it easy for the most part."

"That's what's up bro," Derek says. "I've been doing the same thing. I really need to find a nice little part-time job or do something where I can make some money."

"I feel you," I say. "I need to do the same thing because it's getting rough out here right now."

"You're preaching now my brother," Derek says. "My mama and I are having a hard time maintaining over here. She's been looking for a better paying job for a while."

"My mama is looking for a better job too," I say. "Her warehouse job is talking about letting some of their workers go for good."

"That's crazy bro," Derek says. "Things got to get better for both of our families."

"We have to make some moves for that to happen," I say. "Sitting on our butts all day isn't going to make things change any time soon."

"We'll come up with something bro," Derek says. "Surviving is what we do best. We'll eventually figure it out."

This is one of the best things I like about my homie Derek. He's always positive no matter what's going on and he helps me keep my spirit up during tough times. It's good to have people in your circle like that. Derek is really a good person at heart. I don't think I could even wish for a better best friend.

"Are you ready for school to start back?" I ask.

Derek's face lights up. *"You better know it,"* he says. "It's our senior year and I'm ready to graduate. It's been a long time coming. I'm sure prom will be off the chain this year too. Do you have anybody in mind you want to ask to the prom?"

"There's nobody in particular right now," I say. "You know getting a date has never been a problem for me anyway."

"I hear you Mr. Denzel Washington," Derek says. "I can't wait to see how this will unfold. Good luck my guy."

"I don't need any luck. You'll see. Are you taking anyone to the prom?"

"Yeah, but I don't know who it'll be just yet. I'll be considering all my options when school starts back. You know the ladies can't keep their hands off me."

"I hear you Derek."

It appears that Derek has somehow convinced himself that he's a real ladies' man. I can't even remember the last time this dude had a date. He was trying his best to smooth talk a girl just last week and the conversation ended with him being slapped in the face. It was hilarious.

"You had some really good grades last year bro," Derek says. "You'll definitely be graduating in the top of our senior class. What do you plan to do after graduation?"

"I've had my mind set on going to college for sure," I say. "I'm still thinking about what I want to major in."

"That's good," Derek says. "I'm thinking about taking up a trade. I'll be looking into some more stuff once school is back in session. On another note, let's go grab something from the store."

"I was just about to say that. I could really go for a nice cold drink right about now. Let's roll out bro."

As we navigate through the neighborhood on our way to the store, both of us are sweating bullets. This sun isn't letting up any time soon. I can't wait to get a nice cold drink to my lips. On our way to the store, we pass several drug dealers posted up on just about every other corner. No matter how hot it gets outside, they'll always be posted up on these street corners hustling around the clock.

We finally make it to the store and Derek goes in first. As usual, the store owner Pablo is at the front counter listening to music and doing nothing.

"My main man Pablo," Derek says. "How are you doing my friend?"

"I'm doing well," Pablo says. "What can I help you gentlemen with today?"

"We're just trying to get something to drink and maybe some snacks for later on," I say.

Then Derek says, "We might get one of those cooked pizzas you got over there Pablo."

"Okay gentlemen. Just let me know and I'll hook you guys up with one."

Derek and I head toward the back of the store to get some drinks. Pablo does a really good job by keeping his drinks fully stocked. Whenever I come in here, I always expect for a nice cold fruit punch drink to be waiting on me.

"Will you go half on a pizza with me bro?" Derek asks.

"You wanted a pizza bro, not me," I say. "Do you have enough money to get it yourself?"

"No. That's why I need you to go half on it with me."

"If I go half on it with you this time, you have to buy both of us a chicken plate next time."

"It's a deal bro. I promise I'll pay for everything next time."

I reach into my pocket and give Derek five dollars. I hope he doesn't get amnesia the next time we come back for those chicken plates. We both grab our drinks and make our way to the snack aisle. I may just grab some chips and call it a day. Just when we're about to head to the front of the store to checkout, someone comes busting into the store.

"Put your hands up and step back from the register!" someone yells.

I glance over the aisles and a man is holding up a big gun at Pablo. I can't believe the store is getting robbed with us in it.

"What's going on up there?" Derek asks.

"Somebody is *robbing the store*," I say.

"Oh snap," Derek says, with a frighten look on his face.

I take another glance over the aisles and there's another man with the gunman. Both guys have red and white striped bandanas hanging out of their back pockets. They also have the same colored bandanas tied around their face too. These two

Bluff City Mob gang members are robbing this store in broad daylight.

"We need to keep quiet so they won't hear us bro," I say.

Then Derek says, "You don't have to tell me. I'm about to be quiet as a mouse over here."

As I continue to watch everything go down in the front of the store, the man without the gun goes behind the counter and starts taking money out of the register. I can tell from the look on Pablo's face that he's extremely upset.

"Where's the safe Pablo?" the gunman asks. "We want all those big bills too."

"I don't know what you're talking about," Pablo says. "I don't have a safe."

"Don't play with me right now," the gunman says. "We want all the money that's in the safe too."

"You got to be either deaf or just stupid," Pablo says. "I just told you I don't have a safe."

"*What did you call me*?" the gunman yells.

The other man comes back from around the counter with all the money he took from the register.

Then Pablo says, "You have what you came to get. Please leave now. I don't want any more trouble."

"It's too late for that now," the gunman says.

The gunman fires a shot at Pablo and he falls to the floor. Both men quickly run out of the store. I can't believe this just happened. After a few seconds, Derek and I run to the front of the store. Right when I'm about to look over the front counter, Pablo stands up. It appears that the bullet just grazed his arm, leaving a small-sized cut on the side of his arm.

"Are you alright Pablo?" I ask.

"Yeah, I'm okay," he says. "The bullet clipped me, but I'll be fine. I can't believe that bastard shot at me."

"You're lucky Pablo," Derek says. "That bullet could've taken you out."

"I know right," he says.

Pablo reaches for a towel behind the counter and places it on the bullet wound.

"Let me call the police," Pablo says. "I hope it doesn't take them forever to get here."

Derek quickly pulls me to the side while Pablo is calling the police. He still looks shaken up from the whole thing.

"When the police get here, make sure you tell them you didn't see anything or you didn't recognize those dudes robbing the place," Derek says.

"I'm not saying anything bro," I say. "I don't have time for BCM coming at me for snitching."

"You got that right," Derek says.

"I'm sure the police won't ask us that many questions anyway," I say. "The camera footage from the store will give them all the answers they need."

After a few minutes, the police make it to the store. Just as Derek and I discussed, we both tell the police that we didn't recognize the robbers. Once they're done asking us questions, they tell us we can leave. We exit the store and begin heading back to Derek's house.

"BCM is off the chain bro," Derek says. "They robbed the store in the middle of the day and shot at Pablo like it was nothing."

"You know those dudes don't care about nothing," I say. "They've been running this whole neighborhood lately. Nobody ever messes with them. Even the police hardly ever get at them."

"Have they ever asked you to join their gang?" Derek asks.

"Of course. They try to recruit every young dude in the neighborhood. What about you?"

"I had one of them approach me in the park the other day and the guy was trying his best to convince me to join."

"Have you ever seen them hanging out around the school when school is in session?" I ask.

"All the time bro," Derek says. "They're small in numbers right now, but I'm sure that'll change overtime. More people are bound to join them."

"You're right," I say. "More people will join them, but definitely not us."

We finally make it back to Derek's house. For the next thirty minutes, we sit on Derek's porch and continue to talk about how crazy that robbery was today. I wasn't expecting that at all. Those BCM dudes are dangerous. I hope I never have to experience anything like that again. I'm glad Derek and

I made it out of that store without getting hurt. Things could have been worse.

Chapter Three

I WAKE UP drenched in sweat. I just had a bad dream about the store robbery. It's been a few days since the robbery at Pablo's store went down. I don't see myself going back there any time soon. Maybe I'll start going back there in a couple of weeks. My alarm clock shows 7:25 a.m. I haven't been up this early all summer. I climb out of my bed, slip on my house shoes, and head to the living room. As no surprise, Mama is in the living room sitting on the couch and she still has on her work clothes. I know she's tired.

"Good morning Mama," I say.

"Good morning son," Mama says. "Why are you up so early this morning?"

"I don't know," I say. "Just couldn't sleep any longer. How'd work go last night?"

"It went alright," she says. "Glad to get home and rest my feet."

"That's good Mama. I'm glad you're home too. I think Cameron is still sleeping. I haven't heard him rumbling around yet this morning."

"He'll be up in a couple of hours. I'll start making some breakfast for you boys in a little bit. Turn on the television for me son."

I grab the remote off the table and turn on the living room television. The first thing that pops up on the screen is the news. The news anchor is talking about the robbery that took place at Pablo's store the other day. According to the news anchor, the police still haven't identified the two guys responsible for the robbery.

"That's terrible," Mama says. "This neighborhood is continuing to get worse day by day."

I didn't tell her that Derek and I were at the store when the robbery took place. She has enough on her plate right now and I don't want to add more worries or stress. Plus, if I had told her, she'd probably tell me that I couldn't go back there ever again.

"They'll never catch the two guys that robbed the store," I say.

"You're *probably* right," she says. "The police halfway do their job anyway when it comes to solving cases in this neighborhood."

Then I say, "Too bad that's the closest corner store by our house. The next closest store is about a twenty-minute walk from here."

"That's okay," she says. "I guess you'll be taking that extra walk for a while. I don't want you or your brother going to Pablo's store until things cool down."

"Yes, ma'am. I won't."

I leave the living room and go into the kitchen. It's hot in this house and I could use something to drink. I open the refrigerator and there's absolutely nothing to drink. There's only one pack of smoked sausages and a jar of grape jelly inside the refrigerator. We never have much to eat or drink in this house.

"Let me get started on making some breakfast," Mama says as she walks into the kitchen.

"Uh, how are you going to make breakfast this morning without any food?" I ask.

"I can't *believe this*," she says. "I forgot to stop by the store on my way to the house this morning. Is there any milk in the refrigerator?"

"No, ma'am," I say. "We couldn't even eat cereal this morning if we wanted to. No milk or cereal here."

"I'll go to the store in a few minutes and grab a few things so we can have something to eat," she says. "I can't get much because I barely have enough money for us to make it until I get paid again."

"That really sucks," I say. "How is the job search going?"

"Well—not so good," she says. "I've done a ton of applications online, but I haven't gotten any responses back yet."

"Hopefully, you'll start getting some responses soon," I say.

"Pastor Wright may be able to help me out," she says. "When I get a chance, I'll give him a call today."

"That's a good idea Mama. I'm sure he'll be able to help you find something."

"I'll give it a try. Pastor normally has a few connections with businesspeople in the neighborhood. Keep an eye on your brother while I run to the store."

"Yes, ma'am."

As she heads out of the front door, I go back into the living room and relax on the couch. A few seconds later, the house phone rings. I get off the couch and go answer it.

"Good morning fat head," says a familiar male voice.

"Who is this playing on my phone so early?" I ask.

"It's Derek you fat head fool."

"What do you want this early bro?"

"I'm just checking up on you bro. I was trying to see what you planned on doing today."

"I don't know yet. Trying to figure out what I'm going to eat first. Our refrigerator is empty as usual. Do you all have anything over there to eat?"

"We only got cereal. You're welcomed to come get a bowl this morning if you want."

"That's okay. I appreciate the offer though. My mama just went to the store to grab a few things for the house. She'll be back soon."

"That's what's up," Derek says. "Speaking of store, did you see the store robbery on the news this morning?"

"Yeah, I saw it," I say. "I still can't believe that happened while we were in there. I had a dream about it this morning right before I woke up."

"I'm glad Pablo survived," Derek says. "Things could've been much worse."

"You're right," I say. "My mama told me to avoid going to his store for a while. I'll have to start going to that other corner store that takes forever to get to on foot."

"It's about time for Pablo to put up glass around his front counter," Derek says. "Those guys are bound to rob his store again if he doesn't put it up."

"Pablo is a smart dude," I say. "I'm *pretty* sure he's going to be doing that as soon as possible. I think that was the first time he's ever gotten robbed."

"Where's your little brother?" Derek asks.

"He's still asleep. He should be waking up soon."

"Do you want to meet me at the park a little later today?" Derek asks.

"That's cool," I say. "While I'm out today, I need to go by a few places in the neighborhood to see if anyone is hiring. I really need to get some money in my pocket."

"Me too," Derek says. "My household is really hurting too. We'll figure something out. We both are natural born hustlers."

"I hear you," I say. "We can meet up at the park around twelve o'clock."

"I'll be there," Derek says. "Well—see you then."

I hang up the phone and get ready to take a shower. Hopefully, Mama will be back by the time I finish taking a shower. I need to at least put a bowl of cereal on my stomach before I leave out of the house.

Chapter Four

I ARRIVE AT the park to link up with Derek. There are a few guys shooting dice on the basketball court and a couple of kids riding their bikes through the park. As usual, I spot a few drug dealers roaming around the park trying to help people get their next high. I take a seat on one of the park benches. A few minutes later, Derek walks up.

"I see you made it," Derek says.

"Of course," I say. "Today is going to be another scorching hot day."

"You're right," Derek says. "I can't wait until the winter comes back around bro. I'm getting tired of all these super-hot summer days. I've been drinking tons of water these past few days to stay hydrated. What places were you going to check out for jobs today?"

"I don't know," I say. "I guess everything that's pretty much in walking distance. I wish my bike wasn't broken. All this traveling by foot *really* sucks."

"I know right," Derek says. "What happened to your bike bro?"

"Cameron broke my bike chain about a month ago. He was trying to do some tricks on my bike in our front yard. He had no business on it anyway."

Derek laughs. I can't wait until Cameron get some more money. I'm taking every last red cent he has for breaking my bike chain.

Then Derek says, "That little dude is bad. I'm glad I don't have any little brothers."

"He's not that bad," I say. "Even though he gets on my nerves every other day and gets into things he shouldn't, I can manage to put up with him for the most part. Why didn't your mama have more kids?"

"I'm sure it was because my daddy walked out on us when I was around . . . six years old," he says. "Since then, it's just been my mama and me."

"My daddy walked out on us too," I say. "He left a few years after Cameron was born and never came back. I don't think Cameron even remembers what our daddy looks like."

"Has he ever tried to call you all to see if you're doing alright?" he asks.

"Not at all. My mama never talks about him, so we never ask about him either."

While Derek and I are talking, I notice a nice-looking girl slowly coming our way. As she gets a little closer, I then recognize her with ease. It's Jessica Sutton, one of the finest girls I've ever seen in my entire life. Jessica is tall with long black hair. She has light brown eyes and a very nice physique like a supermodel. The creator has blessed her from top to bottom. This girl is simply amazing. We've known each other for a few years now. She attends the same high school that Derek and I go to. I might try my luck and ask her to the prom this year. It's worth the shot.

"Hey guys," Jessica says. "I haven't seen you all in a while."

"Hey Jessica," I say. "It's been a little minute since we've crossed paths. How is your summer going?"

"It's going good," Jessica says. "I've been cooped up in the house for the most part. I get out of the house every now and then to get some exercise. I have to make sure I keep this body right."

"I must say—you're doing a good job with that," Derek says.

Jessica smiles and says, "Thanks Derek. I try my best. Are you guys ready for school to start back?"

"*Most definitely*," I say. "I can't wait to see what our senior year will be like."

"I'm ready too," Derek says. "We got to go out with a bang our senior year."

"You got that right," Jessica says. "I'm ready to turn-up and finish strong. Over the summer, I've been researching a few colleges that I'd probably like to attend."

"That's good Jessica," I say. "With your good grades, you're bound to get accepted anywhere."

During our conversation, I spot a group of guys out the corner of my eye slowly approaching us. From the looks of it, they're a part of the notorious Bluff City Mob gang. They're wearing their traditional red and white striped bandanas around their heads. As they get a little closer, I notice that Pistol P is with the group. Pistol P is the leader of BCM.

"What's up people?" Pistol P says. "How are the streets treating you all?"

"For the most part . . . not bad at all," Derek says. "How about you?"

"We good over here," Pistol P says. "Everybody knows that we got the neighborhood on lockdown. We're running things and making moves out here."

"That's what we've heard," I say.

"We're being generous by giving people an opportunity to get down with us," Pistol P says. "*Anybody interested?*"

"I think we'll pass my guy," I say. "We appreciate you taking . . ."

"Slow down young fella," Pistol P says. "You all would be passing up on an opportunity of a lifetime! My squad runs this city and nobody around here can mess with us."

"Like my boy Avery said, we'll pass my guy," Derek says.

"I should've known you all were a bunch of little punks," Pistol P says.

"You don't have to talk to us like that bro," Derek says.

"I can talk to both of you young dudes anyway I want," Pistol P says. "If you got a problem with what I said, these guys behind me can take care of that."

"We don't want any problems with you guys," I say. "We're good."

"That's what I like to hear," Pistol P says. "I see you all are hanging out with a fine young chick. She hasn't said a word since I walked up. What's your name baby?"

"I'd rather not tell you," Jessica says. "That's really not important."

"You don't have to be rude," Pistol P says. "I'm just trying to be friendly. Do you have a boyfriend?"

"Not at the moment," Jessica says. "I'm not dating right now. I'm just focusing on myself."

Then Pistol P says, "That's too bad. I'd love to take you out and have a good time. You'll have much more fun with me than hanging with these two guys."

"I think I'll pass," she says. "I'm good."

"You really don't know what you're missing miss lady," Pistol P says. "It's your lost. You could've been hanging with a real man baby. I guess I'll leave you and these little boys alone now. I got better things to do."

Pistol P and his crew finally walks away. Those guys are some real chumps. Pistol P just literally talked to Derek and I like punks in front of Jessica. I hope Jessica doesn't think that I'm a weak guy after what just happened.

"Those dudes are some real jerks," Derek says. "Pistol P didn't have to come at us like that."

"I feel you," I say. "I was just trying to keep the peace so they'd eventually leave. It worked. If we had escalated the situation and they decided they wanted to fight us, we would've been outnumbered. Also, they probably had weapons on them too. You know how gang bangers roll. We didn't need those problems."

"I guess you're right," Derek says. "They'll get theirs one day. I hope I'm around to see it all."

"Me too," I say. "Everybody just started noticing them last year. Pistol P and his brother are the ones who started BCM. How big is the gang now?"

"I heard they have about fifteen or twenty members right now," Derek says. "Those dudes are lame."

"Sorry you had to deal with that Jessica," I say.

"It's okay," she says. "I'm going to continue with my walk. I'll see you all later."

"Okay Jessica," I say. "See you later."

Jessica walks away. Because of Pistol P and his crew, I didn't even get around to asking Jessica for her phone number. Maybe I'll try again the next time I see her. The next time we meet, I hope I can work my magic without any unwanted interruptions.

"BCM messed up the whole groove," Derek says. "You didn't really get a chance to put your moves on Jessica."

"I know right!" I say. "I'll try next time. I know she's feeling me."

"We'll see about that," Derek says. "Let's go to the store bro. I know you're hungry now like I am."

"Yeah—I am. You want to go to . . . *Pablo's store*?"

"Yeah. I know you said your mama told you not to go there for a while. We'll just make it quick. She won't find out bro unless you tell her you've been there."

"Alright. I hope you didn't forget about our deal. Are you paying for both of our food this time?"

"*Relax pimp*. I remember. I got you on this one."

"I can't believe you remembered this time," I say. "You usually get a sudden case of amnesia when it's time for you to hold up your end of a deal."

"Don't do me like that bro," Derek says.

"It's true," I say. "I'm only stating facts."

"I'm coming through on this one. Now, *stop* the whining and let's go to the store. My stomach is touching my back."

After a nice fifteen-minute walk, Derek and I make it to Pablo's store. The first thing I recognize right before we walk inside is the new camera Pablo has gotten installed outside the store. I knew he was going to make some changes after his store got robbed. Once we get inside the store, we both are amazed by the new bullet proof glass that Pablo has gotten built around the front counter.

"I see that you've made some upgrades to the store Pablo," Derek says.

"It was only right for me to do so," Pablo says. "I won't be getting robbed like that ever again."

"Did the police find those guys who robbed your store?" I ask.

"I don't think so," Pablo says. "They haven't notified me about arresting anybody yet. Did one of you by any chance get a good look at their faces or know who they might be?"

"Sorry Pablo," Derek says. "Unfortunately, we didn't see their faces. We have no clue who they were."

"Okay. What can I do for you gentlemen today?"

"Are you selling any fish plates today?" I ask.

"I most certainly am," Pablo says. "Give me a few minutes and I'll fix them for you gentlemen."

"Cool," I say.

"After today, I'll be completely broke bro," Derek says. "My mama won't be able to slip me any cash until she gets paid again next week."

"That sucks," I say. "If you need to hold a few dollars, I got you bro. I got about twenty dollars to my name right now."

"I appreciate it," Derek says. "You always got my back."

"No problem," I say. "You always have mine too."

"We must find something soon to make some money," Derek says. "It would be good if we had something saved up before we go back to school. We can't depend on our mamas for money. They got enough to deal with already."

"True," I say. "I'll be glad if I find a part-time job soon. I'm tired of being broke all the time. This isn't fun at all."

Pablo makes his way back to the front counter with our fish plates. The aroma from the food is making me even hungrier.

"That'll be twelve dollars gentlemen," Pablo says.

"Can we by any chance get that favorite customer discount today?" Derek asks.

"*That's* a good one," Pablo says. "Nobody has ever tried me with that one. No discounts at my store gentlemen. Everybody has to pay in full."

"You can't knock a man for trying," Derek says. "It's rough out here in these streets."

Derek hands Pablo the money for the food and he hands us the fish plates. We leave out of the store in a hurry, anxious to start eating our food right away. We'll have to eat at Derek's house. Can't take the food back to my house because Mama will know where I got it from.

Chapter Five

SCHOOL WILL BE starting back in just a few days. Summer break went by extremely fast, but I'm really looking forward to my senior year of high school. Earlier today, I talked to Derek over the phone and I agreed to meet up with him at the new neighborhood hot wing restaurant. It's just a few blocks from my house. When I arrive at the restaurant, Derek is already present and is feeding his face.

"Slow down on the hot wings bro," I say. "You're eating like you haven't ate anything in days."

"These wings are really good bro," Derek says. "This is going to be our new favorite eating spot for now on."

"If you say so," I say. "From the way you're eating, I guess the wings are on point. You couldn't even wait until I got here before you started eating."

"When I walked into the building and was hit by the good smell of their wing sauce, I had to get something right away. It took you quite a while to get here."

"What flavor did you get on your wings?"

"I got honey-hot and it's definitely on point."

"They look really good and fresh too," I say. "Do you think you can . . . buy me some?"

"Do you have any money?" he asks.

"I'm broke as a joke right now," I say, while patting both of my side pants pockets. "I wouldn't have asked you to buy me something to eat if I had some money on me."

"I'll get you some wings bro."

"*Good looking out.* That's why we're best friends."

"How is Ms. Johnson and Cameron doing?"

"They've been alright. Things could be better. My mama hasn't found another job yet, so things are kind of tight at the house. I think it's starting to really bother her and stress her out. I wish I could do more to help."

"That's messed up. Something has to come through soon."

Then I say, "We've been waiting on that something for a long time now. We've been waiting all summer long bro. Things are crazy right now."

"Keep your head up bro," Derek says. "Better days are to come in the near future."

"Well—I wish those better days would hurry up," I say. "We got problems and issues that need to be handled now."

"Another problem that might be added to your list is BCM," Derek says.

"Uh, why would they be a problem for me?" I ask.

"I've heard that those idiots been robbing people on the streets left and right this past week," he says. "They've been robbing both young and older people in the neighborhood."

"That's insane," I say. "Those dudes are really getting out of control."

"I don't think they're slowing down any time soon either," he says. "I heard that the police haven't even caught or arrested none of those dudes."

"We really need to be careful now when we're out in the neighborhood," I say. "What will we do if we bump into those dudes?"

The gang members of BCM always travel in groups of at least three or more on the streets. In those groups, I'm sure most of them will have either a gun or knife on them. If we bump into them, there's nothing we'll be able to do.

"I'm glad you asked that question bro," he says. "I think we should get a gun of our own."

"Where would we get a gun from?" I ask. "I don't know anybody that would sell us one."

"I got it covered," he says. "I know a guy by the name of Wayne who sells guns for an affordable price on the streets. I've already agreed to meet up with him today at the park."

"Time out," I say. "We both have been broke for most of the summer. Where did you get money from to buy a gun?"

Derek smiles and says, "I took some money from my mama's secret stash the other day."

"You've really lost your mind," I say. "When she finds out her money is missing, it's all over for you bro."

"She won't find out. I'll be able to put most of the money back before the month is over. One of my older cousins said that he'll give me some money next week when he gets paid."

"I hope you're right. If not, she's going to slap the black off you and put you on punishment until you turn eighteen."

"I'm not worried about her. I'm more worried about running into BCM and getting robbed. If we don't keep any protection on us, we're screwed."

Derek does have a point. I've never shot or yet alone held a gun before. I've never liked them at all. I really don't want to be carrying a gun, but we do need some protection with all this madness going on in the neighborhood right now.

Then Derek says, "Because of our last encounter with BCM, you weren't able to vibe with Jessica long or ask her for her phone number. I know that's what you were working on when she approached us in the park that day. I saw the look in your eye."

"You're right," I say. "I was about to ask her for her number before those bastards interrupted our conversation."

"Well . . . school is about to start back soon," he says. "You'll get a chance to ask her for her phone number then."

"That's the plan bro," I say. "I really want to take her to the prom this year."

"I know you do," he says. "To help you start preparing for those needed funds, let's find something that'll help us earn some good money."

"I'm with you on that," I say.

"Here is some money bro," he says. "Get some wings and eat so we can roll out. It'll be time for me to meet up with Wayne at the park soon."

After taking the money from Derek, I go to the front counter of the restaurant and order something to eat. This restaurant is extremely clean on the inside. I know its brand new, but hopefully they can keep it up long-term. Most new restaurants in the hood go down quickly right after their grand opening. Black businesses in this neighborhood need to do better.

Once I'm done eating, Derek and I take our stroll to the park to meet up with this guy Wayne. I've never heard about this guy before, but Derek knows more people around the neighborhood than I do. If it wasn't for Derek, I'd probably spend most of my days cooped up in the house. When we make it to the park, Derek points out Wayne and we head in his direction.

"It's nice to see you Wayne," Derek says. "What's up bro?"

"Nothing much," Wayne says. "I appreciate you being on time young blood."

"No problem at all," Derek says.

"Who is this with you?" Wayne asks.

"This is my best friend Avery," Derek says. "He's cool."

"Okay. Nice to meet you Avery," Wayne says.

"Likewise," I say.

Wayne is much older than us. He looks like he's maybe in his mid or late forties. I can tell that he smokes a lot because his lips are as black as the bottom of my shoes.

"I got what you young guys need," Wayne says. "You got the money Derek?"

"I got it."

"Cool," Wayne says. "Let me show you my collection for today."

Wayne pulls up his shirt and shows us two guns tucked in his waistband. They both look new like he just got them or cleaned them very well. This is my first time really seeing a gun up close.

"These are your two options for today," Wayne says. "I have a Ruger and Smith & Wesson for sale. Which one do you want?"

"They both look nice," Derek says. "Which one is the cheapest?"

"I can let the Ruger go for about seventy dollars today," Wayne says. "How much money do you have to spend?"

"I got seventy-five dollars on me," Derek says. "That's all the money I have right now."

"I guess this one is yours then," Wayne says, while pointing at the Ruger. "I'll throw in some bullets for the extra five dollars you got."

"It's a deal bro," Derek says.

Derek and Wayne both exchange the money and gun. Just as he promised, Wayne gives us bullets with the gun as well. I hope Derek will be responsible when handling this gun.

"*You all are set*!" Wayne says.

"I appreciate you doing business with us," Derek says. "I knew I could depend on you to deliver."

"I always deliver young blood," Wayne says. "That's how I keep a good reputation on the streets. Everybody knows I'm the man."

"I know that firsthand now," Derek says.

"One more thing you guys," Wayne says. "I have to make this clear with everybody I sell to."

"What is it?" I ask.

"If you guys ever get caught with this gun, remember that you didn't get this from me."

"We already know," Derek says. "We'll honor the street code."

"That's good. It was a pleasure doing business with both of you. You all be easy now."

Wayne walks away and strolls on through the park. Derek and I now have a real gun. I never would've thought we'd be getting a gun at the end of our summer break. We can't have this thing in our possession when we're at school.

I'm not about to risk everything I got going at school for a stupid gun.

"I'm going to keep the gun at my house bro," Derek says.

"That's cool with me," I say. "You bought it anyway, so it's only right for you to keep it."

"I know," Derek says. "But I want you to know that it's both of ours. You can get it anytime you want. Just let me know."

"Understood," I say. "Where are you going to put it?"

"I'm going to keep it under my bed," Derek says. "My mama never comes in my room. I think it'll be alright there."

"Are you sure about that?" I ask. "You probably think she doesn't go in your room, but you never know. Mamas are very nosey."

"Trust me on this. She'll never find it bro."

"I trust you. I just wanted to make sure. We can never let anyone find this gun."

Chapter Six

THE FIRST WEEK of school has really been great. I've gotten the chance to catch up with quite a few of my old classmates to see how life has treated them over the summer break. For me personally, one of the best things about school being back in session is the free breakfast and lunch that's served every day. Over the past few months, it's been a struggle at my house when it comes to keeping food in the refrigerator. Mama is still trying to find a new job and I've had to settle for syrup sandwiches on many days when I didn't have any money of my own.

My current wardrobe really needs some help right about now. Since things have been tight at home, Mama hasn't been able to get me any new clothes. I'm pretty much rocking the same gear from last school year and I hope people don't notice it. I've even developed a hole in the bottom of one of my shoes and they're starting to get very uncomfortable.

While going through my locker before class, someone walks up behind me and lightly taps me on the shoulder. I nearly drop all my textbooks right when they tap me.

"How is everything going Avery?" Jessica asks.

"*Everything is copacetic,*" I say, trying to sound as smooth as possible.

"That's good," Jessica says. "Do you like all of your classes so far?"

"I like most of them," I say. "I'm not really excited about the art class I'm taking. I just chose it to help fill up my schedule. Do you like most of your classes?"

"I do. I absolutely love my cosmetology class. I love doing hair. History is my second favorite class so far. We both take Mr. Newman for history during fourth period."

"Yeah, we do. Our history class has been interesting so far. Mr. Newman is a cool teacher. Why do you sit all the way in the back of the class?"

"I don't like to get called on to answer questions in class, but apparently you do. Every time I look up, you're raising your hand to answer a question and you usually get it right smart guy."

I knew Jessica had been feeling me lately. I never doubted it. She thinks I'm smart and I bet she thinks I'm cute too. The perfume she's wearing today smells so good. She smells like a fresh basket of fruit and I wouldn't mind having a peach right about now.

While rubbing my chin I say, "I like the fact that you pay close attention to me in class sometimes. I don't have a problem with it at all."

She laughs. "Don't get the big head," she says while smiling. "Seriously, you really are a smart guy. I see a lot of potential in you. You're going to do well for yourself after high school and I can't say that about most of the other guys around here."

"Thanks for the compliment," I say. "I just try to do my best in everything I do. I want to do some great things after high school. It won't be easy, but I'm willing to work hard to make it happen."

"I like to hear that," she says. "Those are the words of a real man who has a purpose. Keep doing what you're doing. You'll make it happen."

"I most certainly will," I say. "I appreciate your support too."

"Let me get to my next class," she says. "I'll talk to you a little later. Take care until then."

As Jessica walks away, I can't help but to stare at her. She continues to float down the hall with her graceful and sassy walk. Other guys in the hall are staring at her too. It just seems like she gets more beautiful with every day that passes. I got to make her mines soon.

After gathering all my things from my locker, I begin to make my way to my next class. The hallway is jam packed with students. On my way to class, I bump into Derek.

"Today has been a really good day for me bro," Derek says with a grin on his face. "I made ten dollars off a card game at the end of lunch today."

"You're crazy," I say. "How were you able to play cards at lunch and not get caught by any teachers or staff?"

"*Easy bro*," he says. "There's always a lookout at the table while the card game is going on. Plus, it's not that many staff members or teachers in the cafeteria during lunch. They can't watch everybody at the same time."

"That's true," I say. "My lunch period has been super packed every day and it's hardly enough tables for everybody."

"It was like that last year," he says. "I'm not surprised it's like that this year too."

"I just finished talking to Jessica a few minutes ago," I say. "She's really feeling me bro."

"Did you get her phone number?"

"Not yet. I should've gotten it today. I'll get it soon for sure."

"You better hurry up on that," he says. "Somebody might slide in and get close to her before you do. A girl that's fine as she is won't be single too long."

"I got it totally under control," I say.

"If you say so," he says. "Go to class bro. I'll see you after school."

"Okay. See you then."

Right after school, Derek and I head to my house. We both have a ton of homework we need to start on. As we're walking down an alley not far from the school, I notice a guy from a short distance walking in our direction. Derek isn't really paying attention to the guy coming our way. He's too busy bragging about all the girls that were flirting with him at school this week. As the guy gets closer to us, I notice a red and white striped bandana hanging out of his front pocket. It's another BCM member roaming the neighborhood in the middle of the day.

"Can you all help me with something?" the guy asks.

"I don't know bro," Derek says. "What is it?"

"I need a few dollars to hold," the guy says. "Can you all help me out?"

"I don't even *know you* like that!" Derek says. "I can't help you with nothing."

At this point, Derek still hasn't realized that this guy is a BCM member. I'm beginning to sense that this isn't going to turn out nice.

"You don't have to be like that," the guy says. "Better yet, both of you can just give me everything you got in your pockets."

Derek and I both look at each other for a split second. Suddenly, the guy pulls up his shirt to show us the gun in his waistband. This isn't how I wanted my afternoon to go.

"You really don't have to do this," I say.

"We don't even have much," Derek says. "Both of us are broke."

"I don't want to hear that," the guy says. "Empty all your pockets right now or get shot. It's your choice."

"*Be cool*," I say. "We'll empty our pockets."

"Wise choice," the guy says. "I knew both of you kids were smart. Now, hurry up!"

I begin to take everything I have out of my pockets and so does Derek. From the look on Derek's face, I can tell he's extremely angry right now. I just hope he goes along with everything and doesn't say something that'll get us shot.

"Wow! I see you all weren't lying about being broke," the guy says. "That little fifteen dollars isn't much, but I'll take it. Something is always better than nothing."

Derek hands the guy his wrinkled up ten-dollar bill first. Then, I hand the guy my last five dollars. He looks at the money for a few seconds and puts it in his pocket.

"Thanks fellas," the guy says. "If we meet again under these circumstances, I expect more money from both of you. BCM runs this city and don't you forget that."

The guy gives me a light shove and walks away laughing. This is really messed up. We've never been robbed before until today. It's not even safe walking home from school anymore. I'm really getting tired of BCM now. These guys are making life harder for me.

"I can't believe this crap!" Derek says, holding his hands on his head. "This man just robbed us! This is crazy."

"I was afraid he was going to shoot us," I say. "I *hate* those dudes."

"I wish I had that pistol on me," Derek says. "It wouldn't have gone down like that."

"I'm just glad it's all over now," I say. "We don't need to cut through any alleys anymore when we're walking home from school."

"You got that right," Derek says. "Going through these alleys is a problem."

"Let's just get to my house bro," I say. "I just want to relax after all of this."

About twenty minutes later, we finally make it to my house. Derek and I are sitting on my porch, still in total shock about how we got robbed right after school. That was crazy.

"I'm keeping that pistol with me more often now," Derek says. "I can't be getting robbed bro. This stops *right* now."

"I agree with you one-hundred percent," I say. "It'll come in handy at times. Just promise me you won't take it to school."

"I won't bro," Derek says. "But I'm *definitely* taking it with me everywhere else I go when I'm not at school. These knuckleheads in these streets got me messed up."

"We'll be good bro," I say.

"We really should try to find the guy that robbed us today and settle the score," Derek says.

"Let it go Derek. It's not worth it. It's over and done now. We just need to move on from it."

"I really don't want to let it go. We can't be letting people *slide* with getting over on us like that. To me, that'll make us look like punks. Do you understand where I'm coming from?"

"I understand what you're saying, but we don't need to worry about that guy anymore. From this point on, we'll just keep the pistol with us and handle our business when it's necessary. Let it go bro."

"I won't go searching for that guy," Derek says. "But if we happen to cross paths again on the streets, I'm handling my business on the spot."

Chapter Seven

ANOTHER WEEKEND HAS arrived. It'll be hard to enjoy it with these empty pockets of mine. On a more positive note, my grades are looking very good after these first four weeks of school. I'm determined to keep it up throughout the entire school year. I must take care of business and make Mama proud. Coming across some money this weekend would be a blessing. I really need some new clothes and shoes. I guess I'll try my luck today and see if Mama has any extra money to give me.

I walk into the living room and Cameron is sitting on the couch. He's eating a big syrup sandwich while watching television. I'm pretty sure the remote control will be good and sticky as usual when he's done with it.

"Where's Mama little man?" I ask.

"I don't know big head," Cameron says. "She was in here with me a little while ago. She's around here somewhere. Do you have any money I can borrow Avery?"

"Sorry little man," I say. "I don't have any money at all. That's why I'm trying to find Mama. I hope she has some money to spare."

"Good luck with that," Cameron says. "I've already been in her room this morning to see if I could find any money on her dresser or under her bed."

"You know you shouldn't be in Mama's room snooping around like that," I say. "If she catches you doing that, it's all over for you."

"She won't catch me. I'm too smooth for that big bro."

"If I catch you, I'm telling Mama. Stop snooping around in her room Cameron."

"You've always been a tattletale. You really got to do better big bro. You're too old for that now."

"Well—somebody has to make sure you stay in line around here."

"Go find Mama big head. You're really killing my vibe right about now."

"I think you've had too many syrup sandwiches," I say. "All that sugar is going straight to your head."

"I'm good big bro," he says. "Do you want to take a bite of my sandwich?"

"I've had enough of you this morning," I say. "Let me go find Mama so I can get out this house."

"Give Mama the mail when you see her," he says. "It's right there on the table."

I grab the mail off the table. As usual, we got a few coupons and a ton of bills. The utility bill has the word urgent in bold red caps on the front of it. I open it up to see what it's about. The utility company has sent us a cutoff notice. The letter states that if Mama doesn't pay the utility bill in seven business days, the company will turn off our utilities until a full payment is made. I need to ask Mama what's going on.

I look out the window to see if Mama is on the porch, but she's not there. I continue to look around the house for Mama, but she's nowhere to be found. She's not in the bathroom, kitchen, or her bedroom. While in the hallway, I begin to hear what sounds like music coming from the back of the house. As I walk to the back of the house and unlock the back door, I spot Mama sitting in a chair in the backyard. She has a small radio in her lap and she's smoking what looks like a joint.

"What are you doing Mama?" I ask. "Is that *marijuana*?"

"Yeah," she says. "You've caught me red-handed son. I'm just trying to calm my nerves right now. I got a lot on my mind."

"This isn't like you at all," I say. "How long has this been going on?"

"I usually don't smoke son," she says. "When certain problems and issues begin to really take a toll on me mentally, this is the one thing that gives me temporary relief and relaxation. I've had a lot to deal with lately."

"I know you've been having a tough time lately Mama. I see it in your face every day."

"I don't want you boys to ever worry about me. There are a lot of things going against us right now, but I'll figure everything out."

"I saw the cutoff notice the utility company sent us in the mail this morning. Are you going to be able to pay the bill in time?"

"Honestly—I really don't know right now son. I won't get another paycheck until two more weeks. I think I'm going to reach out to some of my friends or our relatives to see if anyone can let me borrow the money."

If our utilities get turned off, that would be awful. Just the possibility that it could happen is really starting to worry me. I highly doubt any of our relatives who stay in town will help us out. They hardly ever call or even come visit us.

"I'd gladly give you the money if I had it today Mama," I say. "I hate to see you struggling and worried."

"I know you'd help me if you could son," she says. "But don't you worry about me. I'm going to be just fine. We're going to be okay."

"If you say so Mama," I say.

"Is your brother still in the living room watching television?" she asks.

"He was a few minutes ago before I came back here looking for you," I say.

"Good," she says. "This was the one place I knew I could hide from Cameron. He doesn't like coming in the backyard. I never want Cameron to see me smoking like this. I never wanted you to see me smoking either, but that's over now."

"Your secret is safe with me Mama. I won't tell nobody. But I do wish that you'd stop smoking for good."

"I will son. I'll get it right. Now, go on back in the house for me. I don't want your brother looking for us. I'll be in there in a few minutes."

"Okay. I love you Mama."

"I love you too son. Now, go back in the house."

I go to my room and start putting on my shoes. I could really use some fresh air right now. I can't help but to worry about what's going to happen next in this house. Are we really going to make it? For the most part, it sure doesn't seem that way. Even Mama is in a panic right now. After I get my shoes on, I leave out of the front door in a hurry. The one person I know that'll listen to my problems right now is my boy Derek.

After a brief walk around the block, I make it to Derek's house and knock on the front door. Derek answers the door with his shirt off and he's sweating heavily.

"I was just about to call you in a few minutes bro," Derek says. "I need to get out this house."

"What's going on with you?" I ask.

"*You won't believe this,*" he says. "Both of our air conditioners just stopped working this morning. I've been sweating like a slave in here for the past few hours."

"Wow! Now that's crazy," I say. "For a minute, I thought you had your shirt off because you were in the house exercising. I was just about to tell you to put that bird chest back in the cage bro."

"Whatever bro," he says, lifting his arms and flexing his muscles. "You wish you were built like this. Don't hate on me dude."

"One thing I've never been is a hater," I say. "I'm just telling it like it is."

"Let me grab a shirt," he says. "I'll be right out in a minute."

I take a seat on Derek's front porch. A few minutes later, he comes outside.

"What's been going on bro?" he asks. "From the look on your face, I can tell that something is bothering you."

"*Man* . . . it's a lot going on at my house," I say. "I wish things would get better for my family."

"What's the problem?"

"Our utilities will probably be turned off soon. We got a cutoff notice in the mail this morning. My mama doesn't have the money right now to pay the bill. Plus, she doesn't get paid again until two more weeks."

"I really hate to hear that bro. That's terrible."

"My mama is really stressed out too. Between you and me, I caught her smoking some weed this morning in the backyard."

"That doesn't even sound right. Ms. Johnson is a *weed smoker*?"

"She said she doesn't smoke that often and I believe her. She said she only use it to relax her nerves when a lot of problems come about."

"That's sad bro," he says. "Single mothers *always* have the toughest time keeping a household stable. It's a lot trying to pay all the bills and take care of kids with no help."

"I just wish I could do something," I say. "I don't want our utilities to get turned off."

"If they get turned off, I'm here for you," he says. "If you need to come by and take a shower or need something to eat, just let me know. I'm sure my mama won't mind."

"I appreciate that," I say. "That's really good to know and hear."

"Do you want to go to the park for a little while?" he asks. "Let's go hang out and take your mind off everything for a little bit. You really need it bro."

"That's cool with me," I say. "Let's go."

Once we get to the park, Derek and I head straight to the basketball court to shoot some hoops. A few guys are already on the court going at it like hoop stars. We quickly let the guys on the court know that we got next against the winner of their game. While we're watching the guys finish up their game from one of the park benches, Wayne walks up and sits next to us.

"I see you fellas are waiting to get on the court next," Wayne says.

"You bet," I say. "Derek and I run this court. Nobody in this neighborhood can beat us."

"I like to hear that young blood," Wayne says. "I haven't seen you all in a while. We haven't bumped into each other since the last time we conducted business. How are things going?"

"Things aren't so good right now," Derek says. "Avery and I both need to make some money. The struggle is real out here."

"I hear you," Wayne says. "If you guys really want to make some easy money, I might be able to help with that."

"Oh really," I say. "How can you do that Wayne?"

"Both of you should know by now that I'm an all-around hustler. I do some of everything out here in these streets. I dabble a little bit in the weed game to make some money. If you guys want, I could supply you all with some weed to sell to make money."

My mama would kill me if she knew I was selling weed. From the look on Derek's face, I can tell he's very interested in what Wayne is offering us.

"How much money would we make doing this?" Derek asks. "We don't have any money right now to even buy some weed from you."

"No worries young blood," Wayne says. "For now, I can start you all off with a small amount of weed. When all of it is sold, just give me half of the money you all made from it. Then, you'll have some money in your pocket to work with. After that, you all can start buying it from me and then sell it at your own price to make a profit. It's that simple."

"That doesn't sound bad at all," Derek says. "What do you think Avery?"

"I don't know bro," I say. "Selling weed has never been something I wanted to do."

"Our pockets have been low for quite some time and you could really use the money. You've been saying that you want to help your mama out with the house. Now is your chance to do it. How else are we going to make money right now?"

"Doing this would be very risky," I say. "I don't want to go to jail no time soon. I got a real future to be thinking about."

"Pushing this work is *easy* young blood," Wayne says. "I've been doing it for a while and I've never had any problems. You won't get caught by the law if you operate in a smart way. Both of you need to get on this money train for real."

"*Come on Avery*," Derek says. "Let's do this bro and get paid. You'll be able to help your family. You can take all that pressure off your mama now."

Derek does make a good case. With everything going on at my house, taking this opportunity would help a lot. We hardly ever have any food at home and we're on the verge of being without utilities. I can't take all this worrying and stress anymore.

"We'll do it Wayne," I say.

"That's what I'm talking about bro!" Derek says. "Let's get this money!"

"Well—it's on now," Wayne says. "I'll meet back up with you all a little later today so we can get started on making this happen."

"That's cool," Derek says. "We really appreciate this offer Wayne. Thank you."

"No problem young blood," Wayne says. "Let me get back to my rounds. I'll see you all later."

After Wayne walks away, Derek gets up from the bench, stands in front of me, and starts clapping his hands. I guess this is his way of thanking me for agreeing to do business with Wayne.

"Sit down bro," I say. "You're doing too much right now."

"I'm just glad you're down with getting this money with Wayne," Derek says. "You had me kind of nervous for a minute. I thought you weren't going to budge."

"A part of me still doesn't want to do it," I say. "But I got to make some money. This is the only available option right now, so I guess I'll take it."

"Everything will work out bro," Derek says. "Just trust me. I got your back and you got mines."

"I hope so. We got to do this the right way Derek. We can't be sloppy with it at all or get too greedy. Understood?"

"Of course. Things will be well organized and on point. I want it to run as smooth as possible. You should be a little excited now. We're *finally* about to make some money."

"I'm a little relieved. Getting this money will help fix many of our problems right now. I'm glad for that."

"It sure will. I'm ready for a change. It's about time for us to reverse this struggle."

Chapter Eight

AFTER JUST TWO weeks, business has been booming. I never thought selling weed at school would take off this fast. The people at school are buying it so fast to the point where Derek and I can barely keep up with the demand. Life has become much better now since I have money in my pocket. I'm able to really help Mama out at home now.

As I walk inside the house, Cameron is sitting on the living room couch and he's hogging the television as usual. He needs to start going outside a little more often to play. He watches too much television nowadays.

"How was school big head?" Cameron asks.

"It was alright today," I say. "What about you?"

"It was cool," he says. "I'm just glad to be home now."

"That's good," I say. "Where's Mama?"

"She's in her room. You might need to go check on her. She was crying a little earlier before you got here."

"Did she say anything about what was bothering her?"

"No. You know she never tells me anything. She told me to don't worry about her. Something is wrong Avery. Please go check on her."

"Okay. I'll go check on her right now."

I walk into Mama's room and she's looking out the window while sitting in her chair. I wonder what's bothering her today.

"Hey Mama," I say. "What's going on?"

"Nothing much son," she says. "I'm just sitting here trying to relax."

By looking at her face, I can tell she's been crying. Both of her eyes are red and puffy. Her tears from earlier have dried up on her face.

"What's wrong now Mama?" I ask. "Cameron told me you were crying earlier."

"Life is just constantly throwing me curve ball after curve ball son. I don't have any money to buy us groceries right now. I don't get paid again until next week. I can't even make you and Cameron dinner tonight."

"Everything is going to be fine Mama."

"Did you just hear what *I said*? I got to figure out how we're going to eat. I can't ask any of my friends to help me out. I already have to pay them back for letting me borrow money last month to keep the utilities on."

"Stop worrying Mama. I got something for you."

I reach in my pocket and pull out some money. Mama's eyes light up like a Christmas tree.

"Here you go Mama," I say, extending my hand toward her to give her the money. "This should be about one-hundred dollars."

"*Wait a minute,*" she says. "Where did you get all this money from?"

I wasn't quite prepared for this question like I should've been. Big mistake on my part. I got to think of something quick.

"Hmmm. I got a job about a week ago. I just got paid today."

"Well—that's new," she says. "Why didn't you tell me you had gotten a job? Where are you working at?"

"I had wanted to surprise you," I say. "I've been working part-time with a cleaning company. I help clean office buildings when they're closed for the day. Someone at school had told me about the job."

"I really would prefer that you not work," she says. "I told you before school started that I wanted you to just concentrate on keeping your grades up. I don't want a job to interfere with you staying on top of your schoolwork."

"I know you told me I didn't need to get a job," I say. "But I promise it won't interfere with my schoolwork Mama. We could really use the extra money around here too. I want to help out if I can and keep some money in my pocket so I can do stuff."

"I guess I'll go ahead and let you continue working," she says. "If any of your grades start to slip, there will be no more working for you son. Is that clear?"

"Yes, ma'am."

"Thanks for the money son."

"You're welcome Mama."

"But listen here son. I don't want you to feel like you're obligated to pay bills around here. Paying bills in this house is my responsibility. Save your money son. If I'm low on cash, then I *might* ask you if I can borrow some money if you have it. Don't just bring money to me like this again."

"Understood Mama."

"I'll go to the store in a little bit and get some food so I can make dinner."

"Okay Mama. Let me go check on Cameron. He should still be in the living room watching television."

I give Mama a big hug and head back to the living room. I hate that I just lied to her about working for a cleaning company. I've been working and making money, but it sure isn't legit at all. For now, selling a little weed is the best way I can make some money. I won't make this a long-term thing. Hopefully, Derek has the same mindset about this whole thing too.

"Mama is going to the store in a little bit Cameron," I say.

"That's what's up," he says. "Is Mama feeling better now?"

"Yeah," I say. "She's good now. I had a nice talk with her. You don't need to worry about her."

"Okay," he says. "I'm glad Mama is going to the store today. We need some food bad. The refrigerator is empty. It's been like that for a while."

"That's about to change for good around here," I say. "I'll be helping Mama with buying food for the house for now on."

"How are you going to do that? You're always broke big head."

"I got myself a little hustle now. I'll be making some decent money. No more days with an empty refrigerator for us."

"That's really cool bro!"

"I know right. I can buy myself some new clothes now and get you some stuff too."

"Can you get me some new shoes when you get some more money?" he asks.

"I sure will little man," I say. "We'll go shopping next weekend to get some new gear."

"Okay. I'll put it on my calendar. I think I'm available for next weekend."

I laugh. Who does this little boy think he is? He surprises me every day with the words that come out of his mouth. I'm sure I was the same way when I was his age. Mama always says that I talked like a grown man sometimes when I was a little kid.

"Is Derek coming with us when we go shopping?" he asks.

"I don't know," I say. "I'll ask him if he wants to come. Most likely, he'll be able to hang out with us."

"Okay," he says. "If he does come, please tell him to do something with his hair."

"What's wrong with his hair?" I ask.

"Every time I see him, his hair is pretty jacked up," he says. "It's always standing up all over his head. He needs to do something with it."

"It does not," I say. "He's in the beginning stage of growing some dreads. In my opinion, I think he does a good job with keeping his hair up to part."

"I don't know what you're looking at when you see him. It always looks like a bunch of tangled up baby spiders on his head. I don't want him embarrassing me when we go to the store next weekend."

"Chill out little man. I'd love to see you tell him that to his face. I don't think the outcome would be pretty for you."

"Hmmm. I don't think it's necessary for me to tell him. I'll let it go."

"That's what I thought tuff guy."

"Are you going to the store with Mama?" he asks.

"No—I'm good," I say. "I'll be here just chilling until she comes back to the house. If you plan on going to the store with her, you better put on your shoes."

"You're right," he says. "Let me get up and go do that now. She'll need a man like me to help her carry the grocery bags."

"You're such a gentleman Cameron," I say, holding my hand to my chest. "Mama has done a great job raising you."

"You need to be going to help me carry the bags too big head."

"You can handle it little man. Before I start watching television, I'm going to get up and go clean the kitchen for Mama. I'll have all the dishes cleaned so Mama can start cooking as soon as she gets back."

"Good thinking big head."

"You know I'm the man!"

Chapter Nine

THINGS REALLY SEEM to be getting better these days. Selling weed is something I'd rather not do, but it helps me keep money in my pockets and take care of home. Over the past few weeks, my clientele at school has continued to increase and money is steadily rolling in just about daily. Life is good.

After making my usual rounds for the day, I make my way to the library after school. Regardless of whatever I got going on these days, staying on top of my schoolwork is always priority. I look at education as my first-class ticket out of the ghetto. While sitting down in the library, my history teacher Mr. Newman approaches me.

"How is everything going son?" Mr. Newman asks.

"I can't complain Mr. Newman," I say. "Everything has been going just fine."

"That's good," he says. "What are you working on?"

"Just a few assignments that are due soon," I say. "One of them is an assignment I have to turn in for your class."

"I like that you're on top of your work son," he says. "You're doing really good in my class so far. Keep up the good work and effort."

"I will," I say. "That's the plan."

"If you have any questions about the assignment before it's due, don't hesitate to ask me," he says. "My door is always open."

"If I do, I will Mr. Newman."

"What are your plans for college? Have you started applying for schools yet?"

"I've been looking and doing research on a few colleges. I haven't applied to any yet. I haven't figured out what I want to major in just yet."

"Okay. I just wanted to make sure that you at least got the ball rolling with trying to map out your future. You're a smart young man and I know you'll do well in college."

"Thanks Mr. Newman. I'll have everything figured out soon about college."

"If you need any help with applying for college or looking for information about college, just let me know. I can help you with that when I'm available."

"Okay. Thanks for looking out Mr. Newman."

"No problem at all son. I'll let you get back to working on your assignments. I'll see you in class soon."

Mr. Newman walks away and leaves out of the library. Once I've completed as much as I can for one day, I pack up my things and head home. When I finally make it home, I walk inside the living room and Cameron is on the couch crying.

"What's wrong with you little man?" I ask.

Cameron wipes his face and says, "Mama is hurt Avery. She's hurt really bad."

"Where is she?" I ask.

"She's in the kitchen," Cameron says. "She called the police a few minutes ago. They should be on the way."

With my heart beginning to race fast, I try my best to stay calm and quickly make my way to the kitchen. When I walk inside the kitchen, Mama is sitting down and she's holding a towel to the front of her head. She's bleeding right above her right eye.

"*What happened to you Mama?*" I ask.

"I'm alright son," she says. "A bunch of young thugs just robbed me right down the street. They took all the money I had on me."

"I can't believe this happened!" I say. "Cameron said you already called the police. Did you?"

"Yeah," she says. "They'll eventually get here soon. You know they're slow when it comes to responding to stuff around here."

"Can I do anything for you Mama until they get here?" I ask.

"Just get me a glass of water and go sit with your brother until the police gets here. He's really scared right now. Try your best to calm him down for me."

"Okay."

I fix Mama a glass of water and then head to the living room to sit with Cameron. About twelve minutes later, someone knocks at the front door. The police have finally arrived. I open the door and a tall white male officer is on the porch.

"Good evening," the officer says. "I'm responding to an emergency call from this residence."

"My mama was robbed down the street a little while ago," I say. "She made the emergency call. She's sitting in the kitchen now. You can come in, sir."

The officer walks in and I lead him to the kitchen. Mama has taken the towel off her head. She has a nice size cut above her eye.

"Hello, ma'am," the officer says. "I'm responding to your emergency call. Do you need any medical attention right now?"

"I'm fine, sir," she says. "I have a small cut on my head, but the bleeding has slowed up."

"What's your name, ma'am?" the officer asks.

"My name is Sophia Johnson."

"It's nice to meet you Ms. Johnson," the officer says. "Can you tell me what happened to you?"

"I sure can," she says. "I was almost to my house when these two guys walked up to me asking if I had any money to spare. I told them no and then they both started cussing me out. I told them to leave me alone. I wasn't about to argue with them. Right when I was about to turn away from them, one of the guys hit me in the head with a glass bottle. I fell to the ground and the guys grabbed my purse. They took all my money out of my purse, threw my purse back at me, and walked away."

"Did you get a good look at the two guys?" the officer asks.

"They both were young black males," she says. "I think they were in their mid or late twenties. They both were very tall and had low haircuts. I've never seen them before until this happened today."

"Is there anything else you can tell me about the two guys? What were they wearing?"

"They both were wearing long white t-shirts and baggy blue jeans. Also, when they were walking off, I noticed they both had a red and white striped bandana hanging out of their back pockets."

This doesn't surprise me at all. Mama has gotten robbed by two BCM members. These dudes are robbing everybody in the neighborhood.

"Thanks for that information, ma'am," the officer says. "It appears that you may have gotten robbed by two gang members. Can you come by the station to look at some pictures to see if you can identify these two guys?"

"I can do that," she says. "Can I come by the station first thing tomorrow morning? I *really* just want to get some rest for the remainder of the day."

"That's fine," the officer says. "Someone will be able to assist you when you come in. Just give them the incident number. I'll write it down for you."

The officer writes down the incident number on a piece of paper and hands it to Mama.

"I have a question to ask you," she says.

"Go right ahead," the officer says. "I'm listening, ma'am."

"Why did it take so long for you to get here? You arrived about twenty minutes after I called everything in."

"I can't really give you an answer on that, ma'am. I just came as soon as the dispatcher told me to come check everything out here."

"It's a shame how long it takes the police to respond to emergencies in this neighborhood," she says. "If I had been shot, I probably would've been dead by the time you got here."

"Well . . . I'm glad you didn't get shot," the officer says. "We try our best to respond to all emergencies as quickly as possible. That goes for all the neighborhoods and communities within the city limits."

"I have to disagree with you on that," she says. "The police respond *very* slow to all the black neighborhoods in this city. The predominantly white neighborhoods don't have this problem."

"I'm sorry you feel that way, ma'am," the officer says. "If you want, you can . . ."

"My mama is speaking facts!" I say. "It's not just a feeling she has, it's the truth!"

The officer looks at me and gives me a hard stare. He knows that Mama and I are telling the truth.

"Listen here boy," the officer says. "If you and your mother have a problem with how the police respond to calls in this neighborhood, I suggest you take it up with the mayor's office."

"Who are you *calling boy*?" I ask.

"I'm not about to go there with you," the officer says. "I've told you all who to contact to discuss the issue. I can't help you with that. Is there any more information you all can give me regarding the incident from today?"

"No—that's all," Mama says. "I'll be down to the police station in the morning like I said."

"Okay," the officer says. "I'll be on my way now."

"You do that," I say.

The officer makes his way out of the house onto the front porch. Before he reaches the last step at the bottom of the porch, he turns around and looks at Mama and me.

Then the officer says, "You people can be hard to deal with sometimes. Believe it or not, it's black people that are destroying this city. You people have to do better."

Mama puts her hands on her hips and says, "You're being really disrespectful right now. That's not how a public servant should talk to people. *Shame on you*. Get off my property right now!"

The officer smirks and says, "You all have a wonderful day."

The officer gets in his squad car and drives away. If we ever call for the police again, I hope he won't be the one who comes to our house. That officer is a straight-up racist.

Mama and I go back inside the house and sit on the couch with Cameron. He's finally stopped crying, but I know he's still a little scared because of everything that's happened.

"Are you alright Mama?" Cameron asks.

"I'm fine now baby," she says. "I just have a little cut on my head. I'm okay though."

"Why did those men do that to you Mama?" Cameron asks.

"They were bad men baby boy. Bad people will do bad things to others. We just have to try our best to avoid them when possible."

"Mama is right Cameron," I say. "But there are some good people out there in the world. All people aren't bad and evil. We just have to be careful."

"It's too many bad people in this neighborhood Mama," Cameron says. "There's always shooting going on around here and I'm tired of it. Can we move now?"

"It's not that easy for us to move Cameron," she says. "I don't have the money for us to do that right now. We'll move eventually, but it's going to take some time."

Mama has been singing that same song for three years now and we still haven't moved. I don't even ask her anymore if we're going to move. Cameron will finally get the picture soon too. It's not Mama's fault we haven't been able to move. She really does her best to take care of us, but I know she can only do so much since she's raising us by herself.

"We're going to be alright Cameron," I say. "We won't be living in this neighborhood forever."

"Do I need to get a job to help out Mama?" Cameron asks. "I can help us get some money to move."

Mama smiles and says, "No. You don't need to get a job Cameron. You're not old enough to get one anyway. I got everything under control. I'll let you know when it's time for us to move."

"Okay Mama," Cameron says. "But don't try to say later on that I didn't want to help out."

"She won't," I say. "That'll never come out of her mouth little man."

"Whatever dude," Cameron says.

Cameron gets up from the couch and runs off to his room. Even with all the positive talk we just had, I can tell that Mama is really stressed out by the look on her face.

"Don't worry Mama," I say. "Everything will work itself out."

"I really hope so," she says. "Now that I don't have any money, everything is messed up."

"I'll try to help out the best way I can," I say. "I got some money coming in."

"I appreciate it son," she says. "I don't know what I'd do without you."

It breaks my heart to see Mama like this. Just when things seem to be getting better for us, we get knocked back down.

Chapter Ten

EVER SINCE MAMA got robbed last week, it's been hard for us. I gave Mama all the money I had to help cover the bills for the house. After paying all the bills, we're still left with an empty refrigerator. The only thing we have in the refrigerator is a jug of water. Even with all the madness that's going on, I'm extremely thankful we still have a roof over our heads and working utilities. We'll be eating plenty of syrup sandwiches until Mama and I get some more money. It's now time for me to ramp up my hustle.

While going through my school locker, Derek walks up to me with a big smile on his face.

"Check me out young boy," Derek says. "I got some more new shoes and clothes."

"You look nice bro," I say. "That's a really dope outfit. You've been buying new clothes just about every week for the past two months."

"I know right!" Derek says. "While we're making all this money, I got to at least treat myself."

"You're doing that pretty well bro," I say.

"How is Ms. Johnson doing?" Derek asks.

"She's doing okay. The cut on her head is healing up just fine."

"That's what's up. That whole robbery shouldn't have happened to her. Somebody needs to get rid of all those BCM guys."

"That'll probably never happen bro. I really don't think anybody has the guts to do that. Not even the police."

"Have the police caught the two guys that robbed your mama?"

"No. I seriously doubt they'll catch them. My mama went down to the police station the day after it happened. We still haven't heard anything else since then."

"I'm not surprised by that at all. If you need to borrow any money bro, I'm here for you. I know you had to give your mama just about everything you had after the robbery."

While Derek and I are talking, I notice that he's gotten some new jewelry as well. He has a new gold chain around his neck that looks very expensive.

"When did you get the gold chain bro?" I ask.

"I got it . . . about a week ago. This thing is dope! I just started wearing it this week. I plan on getting some more jewelry in about two weeks. The girls love it bro."

"I bet they do," I say.

"I've gotten so many phone numbers in the past few days," he says. "It's almost getting hard to keep up with all these girls in my phone."

"You got a cell phone too?"

"Yeah. I had to get one. It's making business a whole lot easier too. You should get one when you get back on your feet."

"I can understand you buying a cell phone, but you need to slow down on all the new clothes and jewelry bro."

"What's wrong with the clothes and jewelry?"

"You're bringing too much attention to yourself. We don't need to be flashy while we're handling our business out here."

"I'm not drawing any attention," he says. "I'm just living bro. We're not bothering anybody, so we're good."

"That's what you think," I say. "People are always watching bro. When they see you showing that you're making a lot of money or they think you're getting too big, they'll start hating on you."

"Nobody is hating on us!" he says. "We're getting plenty of love from many people right now. That's the reason why we have so many customers."

"Some of that love you're talking about isn't real bro," I say. "Much of it is probably fake love. We must be smart with how we move and handle things. We talked about this from the jump."

"Avery . . . you need to relax," he says. "We're good all the way around. We're getting money at a good pace and things aren't slowing down."

It's official. The money has gone to Derek's head now. He's not even thinking straight or comprehending anything that I'm saying to him.

Then I say, "Just keep the new clothes and jewelry to a minimum bro. You're doing too much."

"Listen bro," he says. "I'm going to keep doing me. Chill out with all that."

"I'm done with it," I say. "I just hope you really take in what I'm saying to you."

"Let's switch subjects," he says. "I think we both should start selling weed outside of the school grounds now. The neighborhood is a gold mine bro."

"I don't think that's a good idea," I say. "If we start selling weed in the neighborhood, we'll then be moving in on other people territory. Those are problems we don't need."

"What is up with you today?" Derek asks. "You're acting all scary bro."

"I'm good bro," I say. "What you're suggesting isn't the smartest thing to do. We're doing fine with how we're running things so far. There's no need to change anything."

"I've already made up my mind about it," he says. "I'm going to start selling around the neighborhood after school. You can do what you want. I got to get this money."

"Alright," I say. "Don't say I didn't warn you. I'm not doing it."

"I'm out bro," he says. "I'll catch up with you another time."

Derek walks off as if he was annoyed by our conversation. I really wish he'd get himself together quick. He's drowning in greed and his ego.

On the way to my last class for the day, Jessica stops me in the hallway. She's smelling good as usual. I must do my best to keep my cool because I get nervous sometimes when I'm around her.

"Hey Avery," Jessica says. "How are you?"

"I'm doing good," I say. "You look really nice today."

"Thank you," Jessica says, holding her hands on her hips. "We haven't gotten a chance to really talk in a while. We should hang out sometime and catch up."

I can't believe she just suggested that we hang out. God has answered my prayers. I've been wanting to get some one on one time with Jessica for a while.

"I'm cool with that," I say. "When are you available to hang out?"

"I'm not busy today," she says. "What about after school?"

"That's cool," I say. "Let's do it today!"

"Okay," she says. "I'll meet you in front of the library after school."

"I'll be there sweetie," I say.

Jessica smiles at me and walks away. Now is my chance to really vibe with her and possibly make her mine. I can't wait to tell Derek about this. He's been bragging about how all the girls at school are after him. None of the girls he's mentioned to me can even measure up to Jessica.

As planned, Jessica meets me in front of the library right after school. We both decide to hang out at the local ice cream shop a few blocks from the school. She takes it upon herself to drive us there. I've been so occupied lately that I didn't even notice Jessica was driving now. Once we make it to the ice cream shop, we place our orders, get our ice cream, and find somewhere to sit down.

"How long have you been driving now?" I ask.

"I've been driving for about a month now," she says. "I have my learner's permit."

"That's cool," I say. "I need to work on getting mines."

"It sure comes in handy," she says. "My mama lets me use the car I'm driving now to get back and forth to school and other places. She has another car that she drives every day."

"That's a blessing. My mama doesn't have a car right now. We should be getting one at the beginning of the year. When we get it, I can start practicing on my driving skills and get my learner's permit."

"Okay. I can imagine it being hard for you and your family to get around with no car right now."

"Not really. We do what we can to get around. My mama catches the bus to get back and forth to work. I really don't catch the bus like that. For the most part, I get around everywhere on foot these days."

"I can respect that. Keep doing you."

"Thanks. I definitely will."

"Have you started applying to any colleges yet?" she asks.

"Not yet," I say. "I have a few in mind that I've done some research on. I'm scheduled to meet with Mr. Newman soon so he can help me with completing applications and applying for scholarships."

"That's good Avery," she says. "I'm doing some research on a few colleges as well. I'll be doing applications soon."

"What do you want to major in?" I ask.

"I've been interested in getting into a nursing program," she says. "Either that or social work. I want to help people."

"I can see you doing something like that," I say. "You definitely have the personality and face for it. Most nurses and social workers are really pretty."

Jessica blushes and says, "I figured you was about to say that. Thank you."

"You're welcome. It's no secret that you're the prettiest girl in our whole twelfth grade class."

Jessica is staring right into my eyes and just licked her ice cream very slow. Is she trying to turn me on in this ice cream shop? Let me chill out and keep my cool. I'm bugging right now.

Then Jessica says, "You're really handsome yourself. I like your swag Avery."

"*Oh really,*" I say.

"But there's one thing I wish you'd change about yourself," she says.

As of now, I'm totally thrown off. She just gave me a good compliment a few seconds ago. I wonder where this is going now.

"And what would that be?" I ask.

"You and Derek have become really popular around school lately," she says. "I know all about the weed selling you both been doing."

"That would be correct," I say. "We've been selling weed for about . . . two months now. It's been an easy side hustle for both of us."

"That's the one thing I wish you'd change," she says. "If you get caught selling that stuff, you could be in some serious trouble."

"I know. It's a risky thing to do, but I really need the money."

"Have you tried applying for any part-time jobs?"

"I tried that, but I wasn't getting any feedback from anyone. Selling weed was an opportunity that just came about one day. I didn't have anything else going on at the time, so I just hopped on it."

"Well—I think you should stop selling weed. You're better than that Avery. I'd hate to see you jeopardize your future for something like that."

Jessica is right. One slip-up and everything could go bad for me. That's the one thing I hope doesn't happen while I'm hustling.

"I don't plan on doing it that long," I say. "I just really need the money right now."

"If you say so," she says. "Just know it's going to be kind of difficult for you to get closer to me while you're doing that. I don't want to get caught up in any mess. I live a drama free lifestyle."

"That's totally understandable," I say. "I'll consider stopping, especially if it'll help me get closer to you. Things are just . . . kind of hard for me right now. I'll definitely think about it."

"You do that smart guy," she says. "Don't think too long."

"I won't," I say.

"What are you doing for Thanksgiving this year?" she asks.

"I don't know yet. I don't even know if my mama is cooking for Thanksgiving this year. She hasn't said anything to me about cooking."

"If you want, you're welcomed to come join my family and I for Thanksgiving dinner this year. My family normally cooks a big feast."

"Cool," I say. "Thanks for the offer. I'll let you know if I'm coming or not."

"Okay. We'll be more than glad to have you join us. Just let me know."

Chapter Eleven

THANKSGIVING HAS COME and gone. After deciding not to join Jessica and her family for Thanksgiving dinner, I hope I get another opportunity soon to spend time with her. I know I missed out on some good cooking for sure, but I wouldn't have been comfortable eating a lavish dinner with Jessica's family while Cameron and Mama ate alone at home. Most of the money I've made these past few weeks have gone toward the house, so Mama and I weren't able to get much food to cook for Thanksgiving dinner. We did manage to buy one twelve-pound turkey, two cans of collard greens, and one small pan of cornbread dressing from the store. Mama burnt some of the cornbread dressing, so it wasn't all that good.

Despite the not so exciting Thanksgiving we had, Mama has gotten a sudden urge to go to church this morning. I'm quite surprised we're going to church today, given that we haven't been in about seven months. Mama woke Cameron and I up super early to get ready for church. By the time nine o'clock approaches, we're heading out of the front door.

As we're sitting in church, I suddenly notice that a few people are staring at us. Maybe we're getting the stares because they're trying to figure out who we are. Most of the people in here are pretty much strangers to me. I don't remember seeing most of the people that's in here during our last time attending church.

Cameron taps me on the arm and says, "That girl over there is watching me. I think she likes me."

Cameron points her out. She's sitting on the other side of the church.

"She might be interested in you," I say. "But you need to pay attention to the sermon right now."

"Okay," he says. "I'll just get her phone number after service is over."

"Shhh!" Mama says. "Both of you boys pay attention to Pastor."

As Pastor Wright is giving his sermon, I start to think about everything I've been doing lately. Maybe Jessica was right when we were talking at the ice cream shop that day. Should I stop selling weed to make money? Mama is still struggling with maintaining the house and she needs my help right now. I know what I'm doing isn't right, but it's helping us survive. I got to get myself together soon.

After service ends, Cameron runs off to go find that girl he wanted to talk to. Everyone in the church is standing around socializing. Mama and I approach Pastor Wright.

"Hello beautiful people!" Pastor Wright says. "I'm so glad to see you all this morning."

"It's good to be seen Pastor," Mama says. "That was a great sermon you gave this morning."

"Thanks Ms. Johnson," Pastor Wright says. "I took my time to thoroughly prepare that sermon. I had to make sure I delivered God's word and message to the people the best way I could."

"Well—I'm sure they got the message this morning Pastor," I say. "It really spoke to me and had me thinking about my life."

"That's good son," Pastor Wright says. "Where's the little one?"

"He's around here somewhere," Mama says. "I hope he hasn't gone off too far."

"I'm sure he's alright Ms. Johnson," Pastor Wright says. "He's safe here. It's been quite a while since I've seen you all. I've missed you all dearly. Where have you all been hiding?"

Mama smiles and says, "We haven't been hiding Pastor. Things have just been a little rough for us lately. Finding another job has been difficult for me. I've gotten off track of making sure my family comes to church regularly, but I'm going to do better in the future."

"I'm sorry to hear that things haven't been going well for you," Pastor Wright says. "I do remember a few months ago that my secretary said you called to speak with me. I called you back and left a voicemail, but I never heard back from you."

"I don't know how I missed your voicemail," Mama says. "I should've just called you again when I didn't hear from you."

"That's alright," Pastor Wright says. "We can talk now in person since you're here today. Do you all have time to talk with me in my office for a few minutes?"

"Yes, we do," Mama says. "Let me find Cameron first. If he's doing something that he shouldn't be doing, I promise I'm going to . . ."

"There he is Mama," I say. "He's over there talking to that girl in the blue and white dress."

"Get over here Cameron!" she yells, waving Cameron in our direction.

Cameron quickly runs over to us. He has a huge grin on his face. I'm guessing he scored with getting that girl's phone number.

"Hey Pastor Wright," Cameron says.

"Hey son," Pastor Wright says. "You've gotten taller since the last time I saw you. I bet your mama is feeding you well these days."

"Not really," Cameron says. "We barely have any food at the house."

I look at Cameron and shake my head. Mama looks like she's ready to go off on him. Little man talks way too much.

Mama looks at Cameron and says, "Your brother and I are about to talk to Pastor in his office for a few minutes. I want you to sit right here in this front row until we're finished. Don't move Cameron."

"Okay Mama," Cameron says.

Once we're inside Pastor Wright's office, Mama and I sit down in the two chairs in front of his desk. This is the first time I've ever stepped foot into this office.

"Anyone want something to drink? I have bottles of water in my refrigerator."

"No, I'm cool Pastor," I say. "Do you want something Mama?"

"I'm not thirsty," she says. "Thanks for the offer Pastor."

"No problem," he says. "I just want you all to be comfortable."

"You have a very nice office Pastor," I say.

"Thanks son," he says.

"Is that a picture of you and the chief of police on the wall?" I ask.

"It sure is. I've known him for many years. We went to college together. We have a pretty decent relationship."

"That's what's up."

Pastor Wright sits down and leans back in his big black chair.

"I won't hold you all too long," he says. "I just want to see how I can help."

"We appreciate you taking time to talk with us," I say. "We know you're a very busy man."

"Anything for my church family," he says. "So . . . talk to me Ms. Johnson. How many jobs have you applied for within the last few months?"

"A lot. I've applied for around fifteen jobs online. I try to go by the library at least two days a week to use their computers. We don't have internet or a computer at home."

"I see. As far as education, do you have a high school diploma?"

"I do."

"Okay. I know a few business owners that may be looking for help. They all require their employees to have a high school diploma. I can begin reaching out to them starting Monday morning to see if I can get you something."

"That's fantastic!" she says. "I really appreciate you doing that for me Pastor. Thanks."

"You're welcome," he says. "Is there anything else you want to talk about?"

"Well—I've been having trouble keeping up with my household bills," she says. "Mainly because I haven't been able to find another job. Hopefully, that'll change soon."

"Do you all have enough food to eat on the regular basis?" he asks. "The little one did mention that you all barely have food at home."

"We manage to get by," she says.

"Mama, you're not being all the way straight with Pastor," I say. "Please give this man more accurate facts."

"It's alright Ms. Johnson," he says. "There's no need to hold back at all. Do you all keep enough food at home?"

"Not really," she says, crossing her arms together. "I've tried my best to keep food in the house, but I have to make sure our utilities stay on and the rent gets paid every month. It's hard right now."

"I can understand your frustration," he says. "I'm going to pray for you and your household Ms. Johnson. I'm also going to stop by your house Tuesday evening and bring you all some groceries."

"You don't have to do that Pastor," she says. "I don't want to be a . . ."

"It's okay. I'm able to bless you and your family right now. It won't set me back at all."

"You heard the man Mama," I say. "Let Pastor do this for us."

"Okay," she says. "I'm extremely grateful for all your help."

"It's my pleasure," he says. "I'm just glad that I'm able to be a blessing to you all."

"With everything that's going on, I've just tried to stay strong for my boys," she says. "I love them dearly."

"Just as a mother should," he says. "You're a good woman Ms. Johnson."

"I don't know what I'd do without Avery," she says. "He's been pitching in a little bit to help me take care of things around the house. He took it upon himself to get a part-time job a few months ago."

My heart drops into the pit of my stomach. Why did she sit up here and mention that to him?

"That's pretty big of you son," Pastor Wright says. "I admire that you're doing what you can to help your mom out. Where are you working?"

"I work for a cleaning company," I say, scratching the back of my head.

"That sounds interesting," Pastor Wright says. "How long have you been working with them now?"

"Not long. I've been working for about two months now."

"That's good son. Keep doing what you're doing. God will continue to bless you. Besides your job, how is school going?"

"It's going good so far. I've managed to maintain a high grade point average and I'm looking at a few colleges for next year."

"That's what I like to hear son! You've always been a very intelligent young man. You got the potential to do many great things in life as long as you work hard and keep God first at all times."

"I hear you Pastor. Thanks for the compliment."

"You deserve it son. If I can ever help you with anything, don't hesitate to get in contact with me."

"Okay. I will Pastor."

"Is there anything else you want to talk about Ms. Johnson?"

"No," she says. "That was pretty much everything. You got anything else you want to talk about Avery?"

"No, ma'am," I say. "I'm good."

"It's certainly been nice talking to both of you," Pastor Wright says. "As promised, I'll stop by your house on Tuesday Ms. Johnson to drop off those groceries."

"Okay," she says. "And thank you again."

"Anytime," he says. "You all continue to enjoy your day. I'm going to do the same. It's time for me to get something to eat."

Pastor Wright gives Mama and I a hug and we leave out of the office. I really feel bad now that I've lied to Pastor Wright about having a part-time job. On top of that, I told a lie inside the church. I hope God doesn't strike me down for this one because I surely deserve it. I wonder if Mama has told anyone else that I have a part-time job.

Mama and I make our way back to the sanctuary to get Cameron. After just a short wait, Cameron has fallen asleep on the front pew. We wake him up and head on home.

As we're walking up to the house, I see Derek sitting on our porch. I should've called and woke him up this morning to see if he wanted to go to church with us. It would've done him some good to be there.

"What's going on bro?" I ask.

"Same ole stuff on a different day," Derek says. "Hey Ms. Johnson."

"Hey Derek," she says. "It's nice to see you son. How are you and the family doing?"

"We're doing alright," Derek says. "Just trying to survive like everybody else in the hood."

"I hear you son," she says. "Tell your mama I said hello when you see her."

"I will Ms. Johnson," Derek says.

"Are you boys coming inside?" she asks.

"No, ma'am," Derek says. "I just need to talk to Avery for a few minutes. It won't take long."

"Are you sure son?" she asks. "It's pretty chilly out here."

"I'm positive," Derek says.

"Okay. See you later Derek. Come on Cameron. These boys don't want to be bothered with you."

"I don't want to be bothered with them either," Cameron says.

Mama and Cameron goes inside the house while Derek and I stay on the porch.

"I see you and the family went to church this morning," Derek says.

"We sure did," I say. "It was a really good service this morning. You would've enjoyed it."

"*Man* . . . I can't even remember the last time I went to church," Derek says. "It's been forever."

"Before today, it had been a while since we stepped foot in church too," I say. "Mama got us up early this morning. I was surprised when she said that we were going. What's been going on with you today?"

"I was out making a little money not too long ago," he says. "I told you that it's a lot of money to be made out here in the neighborhood."

"I bet. I'm glad you brought that up. We need to talk about that."

"What is there to talk about?" he asks. "Is something wrong?"

"I think we both should stop selling weed bro," I say.

"Here you go with this," he says. "Everything is going good for us right now. Why do we need to stop?"

"Because it's the right thing to do," I say. "We shouldn't be doing it."

"Miss me with that bro!" he says. "You're not thinking straight. I think going to church this morning got you a little scared. If we stop, both of us will go back to being broke all the time. Is that what you really want?"

"We can try to find some legit part-time jobs to make money bro," I say. "My pastor will be helping my mama find another job. Maybe he'll be able to help us find something too if we ask him."

"There's no telling how long it'd take him to find us something if we asked for help," he says.

"You do have a good point," I say.

"I know I do," he says. "I also doubt we'll be able to get something legit that would pay us the same amount of money we're making now. Making money has come super easy for us so far. Stopping right now would be crazy bro. We hot!"

"Our hot streak may not last long," I say. "Plus, I wanted to only do this temporarily. This was never a long-term thing for me."

"I'm not stopping now!" he yells. "I can't do it Avery! You should keep going. Remember that your mama and little brother are really depending on you. If you stop now, it's all over for everybody in your house. You won't have any money to help pay bills or do anything."

I really don't want to go back to being broke. I don't miss those days at all. Derek is also speaking real facts. At this point, it does seem like everything is riding on my current actions. My family's ability to survive these hard times is resting in my hands.

Then Derek says, "I clearly understand that you want to do the right thing, but we got to keep getting this easy money. I need you to have my back on this. We started this together bro."

I take a deep breath and say, "I got your back bro. You can depend on me."

"Thank you," he says. "We're going to be alright. You'll see."

Chapter Twelve

DURING THIS CHRISTMAS break, I've been on my grind tough. I've even joined Derek with selling weed in the neighborhood. With our increased activity on the streets, Derek and I are racking up a lot of money at a very fast pace. Mama is starting to smile more as of lately and I want it to stay that way. I hate to see Mama when she's depressed or stressed out. Thanks to Pastor Wright, she has a job interview coming up this week. I hope she gets it.

While selling weed to customers as they pass through the neighborhood park, Wayne approaches me. He's wearing a huge green bubble coat.

"I see this weather hasn't slowed you down young blood," Wayne says. "You've been out here just about every day for the past week."

"I can't let the weather disrupt my hustle," I say. "But it is cold out here. I got about two layers of thermals on. I'll be alright."

"That's what's up," Wayne says. "I think it might snow tomorrow. That's what the weatherman said this morning on the news."

"I hope not," I say. "That might slow up my business a little bit. Everything is cool so far."

"You and Derek been making some major moves lately," Wayne says. "I've been noticing all the money you all been getting."

"We've taken our hustle up a notch. We've been hitting the streets hard. Being on break from school is working out just fine. Business is definitely booming for us."

"Are you thinking about committing to the streets full-time young blood?"

"Hmmm. Not really. I'm just going to enjoy this while it last."

"You'll be leaving a lot of money on the table if you don't young blood. It's plenty of it to make out here and I don't see that changing."

"I know. I can live with that. I got other plans for the future."

"I can respect that. But I do have an idea that would probably strike your interest."

"What is it?" I ask.

"I'd like to increase you and Derek's weekly supply going forward," Wayne says, rubbing both of his hands together. "What do you think about that?"

I knew Wayne was going to eventually ask me this. He's been making a lot more money too since Derek and I have increased our activity on the streets.

"I think we're good for now," I say. "But let me talk to Derek about it and see what he thinks. I'll get back to you on that soon."

"Sounds like a plan," he says. "I'll be waiting. By the way, where's Derek?"

"I don't know," I say. "He's probably still at home or maybe out chasing after a girl. You know how he is."

"He's always talking about how all the girls at school and in the neighborhood want to be with him," he says. "It's all in his head young blood."

"I talked to him earlier this morning over the phone," I say. "He told me that he was coming up here to the park to make some money."

"He'll be up here soon," he says. "That dude is never missing out on making easy money."

"You got that right."

"I do want to warn you about something young blood."

"What is there to warn me about?"

"You and Derek need to be careful out here. Other people that are hustling around the neighborhood are noticing how you and Derek are starting to get more customers. Some of them will get jealous and might start beefing with you all."

"I figured that would probably happen since we've been putting in more work on the streets," I say. "I won't be out here like that when school starts back."

"Just be careful. Do you stay strapped up?"

"No. Derek normally keeps the gun we bought from you."

"Do you want another one young blood?"

"I'm good for now," I say. "I'll let you know if I need to get another one from you."

"Just say the word and I'll take care of you," he says. "Let me get back to making some more money today. I'll get up with you later."

After Wayne walks away, I get back to serving more customers coming through the park. As soon as I'm done serving my last customer for the afternoon, Derek suddenly runs up to me in a panic. He's breathing extremely hard. I hope he hasn't done something stupid.

"What's wrong bro?" I ask. "Why are you so spooked?"

"I just . . . shot somebody bro," Derek says. "I had to do it."

"You got to be kidding me!" I say. "What happened Derek? Who did you shoot?"

"Give me a second bro," Derek says. "Let me . . . catch my breath."

I look down and I see blood on Derek's pants and shoes.

Then Derek says, "I was just walking through the neighborhood looking for some business. Just a couple blocks from here, I saw the BCM guy that robbed us a few months ago. He was standing on the corner smoking. I'm sure it was him because I remembered that bastard's face. When he wasn't paying attention, I slowly walked up behind him, shot him in the back of one of his legs, and got on down."

"Why did you do that Derek?" I yell. "If he wasn't bothering you, there was no reason for you to shoot him!"

"I'm not trying to hear that bro!" he yells, pointing his finger at my face. "That dude pulled a gun on us and robbed us! And I told you if I ever saw him again, I was going to handle my business. I meant what I had said."

"I had told you to let that go!" I say. "What you just did was pointless and unnecessary."

"Well—I wasn't going to let it go," he says. "You're my best friend and all, but you can't tell me what to do bro. I did what I had to do. He had it coming."

"Miss me with that crap," I say. "What I had told you to do was strictly for the best Derek. I wasn't trying to control you or boss you around. This isn't good at all."

"It's done now," he says.

"How do you know he didn't see you hanging around before you shot him?" I ask.

"He didn't see me bro. Trust me. I watched him from a distance for quite a while. He was standing on the corner getting high as a kite like nobody's business."

"Did anybody else see you? Is he still alive?"

"The whole block was deserted and nobody was around when I did it. I'm sure he's still alive. I told you I shot him in the back of the leg."

"Because you shot him in the back of his leg doesn't mean he's still alive Derek. You said you took off right after you shot him. He could've bled to death!"

"That dude is still alive bro! End of story!"

"This is crazy," I say. "Look at yourself bro! You got that man's blood all over your clothes. We got to get out of here now!"

"I know," he says. "Come with me to my house."

We leave the park and head to Derek's house in a hurry. Once we're there, we go in through the back door so Derek's mama won't see us. After a minute or so, we realize that his mama is not even at the house right now. Derek takes off the bloody clothes and shoes, puts them in a plastic bag, and gets in the shower.

After Derek is done freshening up, we go outside to the backyard. Derek tosses the bag of bloody clothes and shoes over his fence into the alley.

"I'll walk around to the alley in a little bit to burn up those clothes and shoes," he says.

"I'm still mad at you for doing that bro," I say. "None of this should've happened."

"Relax bro," he says. "I got it covered."

"You better hope that guy you shot doesn't die," I say. "If he pulls through and he saw you before or after you shot him, BCM will definitely be out looking for us to get revenge."

"What do you mean us?" he asks. "I'm the one that shot him. If they happen to find out that it was me who did it, why would they even be looking for you?"

"Because I'm sure those BCM dudes have seen us hanging together," I say. "They know about us. We've been on the streets a lot during this past week slanging and hustling just like them."

"You might be right bro," he says. "I wouldn't want you to get caught up in this, but I'm telling you he didn't see me. That fool was too busy getting high off his own product."

"We both should lay low for a while," I say. "We need to stay out of sight for a little bit until this whole thing blows over. Can you at least do that for me bro?"

"I'll do it," he says. "That sounds like the best thing to do."

"Thank you," I say.

"We'll be missing out on a lot of money while we're laying low," he says.

"I'm sure we will," I say. "But that's not important right now. Staying alive and staying out the way for a little while is most important."

"I've managed to save up a lot of money," he says. "I should be alright for a little while."

"I've saved up some money too," I say. "But I did spend a lot of it this week. I finished up my Christmas shopping and I gave my mama some more money to help out with the house."

"I'm pretty much done with all my Christmas shopping too," he says. "If you need to borrow any money, just let me know."

"I'm good." I say. "I'll make it just fine with what I got now."

"Okay," he says. "I'm just trying to be helpful. Are we good bro?"

"I'm really not in a good mood right now," I say. "You've messed up big time today. I'm about to go home. I've had enough for today."

Chapter Thirteen

I'VE BEEN LAYING low at home for twelve straight days now. This was the first time in the last three years that I've stayed at home for New Year's Eve. Usually, I would've been at somebody's house party having a good time. It was nice to see Mama and Cameron smile when they opened their Christmas gifts. Cameron has been playing with his big train set every day since he opened it. Derek gave me a prepaid cell phone for Christmas. He also gave me a rifle, which was a bit too much in my opinion. The day before Christmas, Derek gave me a big guitar case and told me to only open it when I was alone in my room. I followed his instructions. I opened the case that same day and, lo and behold, the rifle was inside it. I guess this was Derek's way of trying to get back on my good side after what he did recently. Mama would flip out if she knew I had a gun.

I'll just keep it stashed under the house for now so nobody will find it.

While sitting on my bed watching television, my phone begins to ring. It's Derek calling. I guess I'll answer it.

"Hello tough guy," I say. "What's going on?"

"Nothing much bro," Derek says. "I was just calling to check up on you."

"I'm good," I say. "I'm just chilling in my room watching television right now."

"That's what's up," Derek says. "I wanted to let you know that I just started back selling weed in the neighborhood yesterday."

"What happened to our agreement about laying low for a while?" I ask.

"We've been laying low long enough bro," he says. "Yesterday was just my first day back on the streets, so chill out. Before then, I been in the house all day every day just like you."

"I think you still should've waited a little longer before starting back up," I say. "But that's on you."

"Well—I needed to start back making money. I can't let my pockets get too low. I'm not worried about those BCM chumps either."

"You should definitely be worried about them. When you shot that guy, it made the local news Derek. You better be glad he didn't die."

"I told you he was going to make it. I shot him right in the leg."

"You shouldn't have done it at all. I just hope nobody else saw you when everything went down that day."

"Nobody saw me bro. And even if somebody did see me, people in the hood don't snitch like that. Snitches get stiches."

"That's a lie. People snitch and talk all the time. You know that."

"Forget all that," he says. "I don't want to talk about it anymore. I was just calling to see how you were doing bro. You haven't been really reaching out to me lately. Do you like the new phone I gave you?"

"It's cool," I say. "I appreciate it."

"No problem bro," he says. "I really got it for you so that you can conduct business a little better. Just about everybody got cell phones now."

"That's true," I say. "I got to get some more minutes for my phone in a little bit."

"You got to get back on your hustle soon so you can have money to do that," he says.

"Yeah, I know. I'll get back to business in a little while. I'll be alright."

"Cool," he says. "The offer is still on the table if you need to borrow any money."

"I'm good bro," I say. "My phone needs to be charged up. I'll get up with you later."

"Don't be a stranger. Piece out bro."

After I put my phone on the charger, I go to the living room. Mama is sitting on the couch watching television and eating a big bag of potato chips. I bet she's been hiding that bag of chips from Cameron because I don't remember seeing it in the kitchen.

"Those chips look good Mama," I say.

"They taste good too son," she says, licking the chip residue off her fingers.

"Where's Cameron?" I ask. "I haven't heard a peep out of him for a while."

"He's back there in his room," she says. "He's probably taking a little nap. He did get up kind of early this morning. That little boy was up when I came in from work."

"He won't be sleep long Mama," I say. "He'll be back up and running around the house soon."

"I got some good news son," she says.

"What is it Mama?"

"I got a new part-time job!"

"That's great! I'm happy for you Mama."

"Thanks son. I felt that the interview went well the other week. I'm *so* glad they called me back. I called Pastor Wright earlier this morning and thanked him for telling me about the job opening."

"Our pastor is a great man," I say. "He really does look out for people and help others the best way he can. He's the definition of a real pastor."

"He sure is," she says. "That time he brought us those groceries almost made me cry. We never had anyone do that for us before."

"When do you start working the new job Mama?" I ask.

"I start next week," she says. "I'll be working about four days a week at a call center. It won't interfere with the schedule for my overnight job either. This is a blessing."

"You're really going to be tired now," I say. "That's a lot of hours you'll be handling during the week."

"Yeah, it is," she says. "But we need the money son. As of now, I'll need you to watch Cameron a little more often. I need you to make sure he does his homework and eats something after school during the week."

"I can do that Mama," I say.

"You're the best!" she says.

"I know. I'm the man of the house."

"Don't let Cameron hear you say that. I think he'd disagree with you."

I laugh. "I think he'd disagree too. Do we have any cereal and milk left Mama?"

"Yeah. There's still some in the kitchen."

"Cool. Let me make myself a bowl of cereal before I get in the shower."

"There's one thing you need to put on your agenda for later today," she says.

"What would that be?" I ask.

"When I talked to Pastor on the phone earlier, he mentioned that he needed to talk to you soon."

"Okay. Did he tell you why he wanted to talk to me?"

"He didn't say. I told him you had time to talk to him today and he said that was fine. I scheduled you to meet with him at the church today at two o'clock."

It wouldn't have hurt if Mama had at least talked to me about this before making me an appointment with Pastor. She doesn't even know if I had plans today or not.

"I'll be there to meet with him," I say. "Maybe he came across a potential job opportunity for me."

"I doubt that's the reason why he wants to meet with you," she says. "He already knows that you have a job. Speaking of that, you've been cooped up in the house for a while and haven't been to work lately. Is there something going on with your cleaning job?"

I freeze up for a few seconds. I must stay on my toes when Mama brings up me having a real job.

"Business has been very slow lately," I say. "Most of the buildings we clean have been closed for the holidays. Things will pick back up next week."

"I figured that was the reason why you haven't been to work in a while," she says. "Cleaning businesses are like that for the most part."

"Yeah. Can I get to my cereal now and take a shower Mama? I don't want to be late meeting Pastor."

"Go ahead son. Take care of your business."

After I take a shower and put on some clothes, I head on down to the church to meet with Pastor Wright. When I get there, he greets me with a firm handshake and then we go to his office to talk.

"Thanks for coming down to see me at such a short notice," Pastor Wright says.

"No problem Pastor," I say. "Thanks for helping my mama find a new job. She's really excited about it. She really needed it."

"You're welcome son," he says. "I do what I can for my people."

"You're a true blessing Pastor," I say. "What did you want to talk about?"

"I want you to *really* take in what we're about to discuss," he says. "This is a serious matter."

"I hear you Pastor," I say. "Lay it on me. Let's talk."

"I wanted to talk about what you've been doing lately," he says. "I know all about your activity on the streets these days."

I feel like my heart just completely stopped. My palms become very sweaty. This is not good.

"What activity are you talking about?" I ask.

"Don't play dumb with me son," he says. "There's no need for that at all. This is a real man to man conversation. I know about everything that goes on in my neighborhood, including drug activity."

I have no choice but to keep it straight with Pastor Wright. I got a lot of respect for this man. Obviously, he knows the truth now.

"You got me Pastor," I say. "I've been selling weed lately to make some money. I know I need to stop."

"You sure do son," he says. "I'm really disappointed in you. It's so many legal ways to make money out here in the community. Why did you choose to sell drugs?"

"It seemed like it was the only opportunity I had at the moment to make some easy money," I say. "I tried looking for a legit job, but it wasn't working out for me."

"Those streets are very dangerous son," he says. "You're a very intelligent young man and I'd hate to see you lose your life out there in the streets."

"I'm not trying to go out like that," I say. "My initial plan was to only do it temporarily until things got better at home. Mama has really been struggling to keep up with the bills, so I just decided to take a chance with selling weed for a little while."

"How do you think your mama would feel if she knew you were selling weed? It's only a matter of time before she finds out."

"She'd be hurt and devastated," I say. "She might not trust me anymore since I lied to her about having a real job. I'm sorry for lying to you too Pastor."

"I forgive you son," he says. "But this needs to stop now."

"I know."

"I have a suggestion for you son."

"I'm listening Pastor."

"To help you make some money the legal way, I can offer you a job here at the church. What do you think about that?"

"That sounds good. What would I be doing? How much does the job pay?"

"I need someone that's willing to work part-time and clean the church twice a week. I can only offer a salary of eight dollars per hour."

"Okay," I say. "I appreciate the offer Pastor. I'll think about it and get back to you."

"Okay," he says. "I'll be looking forward to hearing from you soon."

"Most definitely."

"I want you to really think about what we discussed today," he says. "You need to change your actions for the best. God is looking for more out of you son."

"I understand everything you're saying Pastor."

"Good. If you ever need to talk, you can call me anytime you want."

"That's good to know," I say. "Because things have been really rough for my family lately."

"You got to have faith during challenging situations," he says. "We all have to face challenges in life. You must seek help from good people and believe that God is always in control. I will continue to pray for you and your family."

"Thanks Pastor. It's time for me to head on back home."

"Okay son. Let me know if you need me."

Chapter Fourteen

I'M SO GLAD that school is back in session. Laying low for the past few weeks hasn't been fun at all. Those long days of just being in the house was really starting to get to me. I haven't been in contact with Wayne for quite some time now. I'm sure he's eager to start back doing business with me. Ever since school started back, all my usual customers have been constantly asking me every day about the next potential arrival date for my new stash of weed. That conversation I had with Pastor Wright really hit home for me, but I desperately need to get some real money.

While walking down the hall, Derek and I cross paths. I can tell that he's back to making a lot of money by his new flashy jewelry. He has a gold watch on his wrist I've never seen him wear before.

"How is everything going bro?" Derek asks.

"Everything is going alright," I say. "From the looks of things, I see you're back to making a lot of money."

"I've been on my grind," he says. "I've been making a lot of cash on the streets bro. You should start back selling on the streets after school."

"I think I'm done with selling on the streets," I say. "I'll let you have it. I might just start back selling at school and that's it."

"You'll be missing out bro," he says. "But if that's what you want to do, so be it."

"It's too dangerous on the streets," I say. "And I still feel some type of way after that incident you had."

"You need to get over that bro. I've *been* over that whole situation and I'm not concerned about it."

"I'm pretty sure BCM is out for revenge after what happened to that guy Derek. They're not going to just let that slide. It doesn't work like that."

Derek puts his right arm over my shoulder and walks me over to the empty stairwell.

"Stop being a scary cat bro," he says quietly. "They don't even know who did it. If they know it was me, why haven't they tried to get at me yet?"

"I don't know," I say. "And you can't be so sure that they haven't found out you did it. Maybe they have a plan up their sleeves. They're not stupid."

Derek takes his arm off my shoulder. I can tell that he didn't like what I just said.

"I can't deal with you," he says. "You're acting like a little wimp right now!"

"*Hold up now!*" I say, raising my voice. "I'm not a wimp Derek, so you can miss me with that and any other weak references you might have about me. Truth be told, you can be just plain *stupid* at times! That's a fact!"

"What did you call me?"

"You heard me!" I say. "You act stupid sometimes. You're the reason why we might get caught up with BCM."

"Man . . . forget you! I don't have nothing else to say to you dude. I'm out."

Derek stares me down for a few seconds and walks away. For all I care, he can stay mad at me forever. He's the reason why I've been worrying about BCM lately. After this argument with Derek, I'm starting to believe that our friendship and so-called partnership may not even be worth it anymore.

As I continue walking down the hallway, I notice Jessica coming in my direction. To my surprise, she looks at me for a few seconds as we get closer in distance and walks right past me without any type of acknowledgement.

"Hold up Jessica," I say, walking fast behind her to catch up.

Jessica turns around to me and says, "I really don't want to talk to you Avery."

"What's the problem?" I ask.

"I guess you never took my advice," she says. "You and Derek are hot in these streets right now and I don't want to be associated with you."

"Don't be like that," I say. "I haven't been involved in selling anything for the past month. I put that on everything I love."

"I don't know if I can believe you Avery," she says. "I just know that you and Derek have become a little more popular on the street for selling that crap."

"I've been out of action lately like I told you. Now, I was hustling at the beginning of the Christmas break, but I put a quick halt to it. That's the truth."

"If you say so. But we had a talk about you selling weed a month before the Christmas break. Do our first date at the ice cream shop ring a bell?"

"Yeah, I remember."

"But you continued to still do it from what you just told me."

"You don't understand Jessica. Things have been a little rough for me and . . ."

"I understand clearly. You're doing what you *think* you got to do like most people. You're living dangerously Avery. There's got to be available alternatives for you other than selling weed."

"I know I've been taking a huge risk with hustling at school and on the streets. I'd hate to get caught up. That's one thing I've been thinking about lately since I took a break from it."

"Are you going to start back doing it?" she asks.

"I can't even lie to you Jessica. I don't know."

"I hope you get yourself together. I really like you Avery, but I can't be involved with you right now."

"Maybe we can . . ."

"I have to go Avery. Bye."

Jessica walks away and never looks back. I've clearly messed up my chances of getting with her now. I hope I can get back on her good side soon.

After I continue walking and turn the hallway corner, a strange guy walks up right in front of me. I've never seen him around the school before.

"Where do you think you're going?" he asks.

"That's none of your business," I say. "Do I know you dude?"

"No, you don't," he says. "But you're about to get to know me very well. Let's talk in the restroom across the hall for a minute."

"I'm good bro," I say. "I don't have time to . . ."

"You really don't have a choice," he says.

The guy reaches into his pocket and whips out a long knife. I guess I should take him serious now.

"You don't have to use that bro," I say, holding both of my hands up. "What do you want from me?"

"I want you to go in the restroom across the hall like I said so we can talk for a minute. If not, I don't have a choice but to use this knife on you dude."

"Okay," I say. "Let's go talk."

"You lead the way," he says.

When I walk into the restroom, a large group of guys are standing around talking. Suddenly, everyone in the restroom starts looking at me and begins to laugh. I have no clue of what's going on. Seconds later, I hear a toilet being flushed in one of the restroom stalls. The stall door swings open and out walks the notorious Pistol P.

"It's very nice of you to join us young dude," Pistol P says.

"I really didn't have a choice," I say.

"You had a choice," he says. "It's good you decided to come on in here. If you didn't, my guy would've given you a fresh wound today. That would've been painful and messy for you. You made the right choice."

"What is this about?" I ask.

"You look like a smart dude," he says. "You should already know what this is about."

"I really don't," I say. "You can fill me in on what's going on."

"You and your buddy Derek been selling weed in my hood without my permission. You've been making a lot of money on my turf."

"*Come on Pistol P,*" I say. "The neighborhood is fair game. Everybody is out there hustling to make some money. And I only did it for a short time."

"You got it all wrong young dude," he says. "I run this neighborhood! Nothing can take place or move on the street without my permission. You got that?"

This man really believes that he owns the entire neighborhood. He wouldn't be so tough without his goons. All they do is kiss his butt and do whatever he tells them to do.

"I hear you Pistol P," I say. "I never intended to disrespect you or BCM. I was just trying to make some money so I can survive."

"Somebody shot one of my most loyal members a while ago too," he says. "It could've been you and your buddy Derek that did it."

"I heard about the shooting. We had nothing to do with that Pistol P. I wasn't even on the streets that day when . . ."

"*Shut up.* How would I know that?"

"It's the truth. I'm just keeping it real with you."

"Well—somebody has to answer for that soon. I'll find out who did it. And when I do, it's over for them. I don't play that crap."

The last thing I want is for Pistol P to find out that Derek was the person who shot that guy. That would be bad for the both of us.

"You're free to go now," he says.

"Alright," I say.

"Wait!" he says. "I just want to clear up one more thing with you so we're on the same page."

"What's up?"

"I don't want to see you or your buddy Derek selling weed anymore on the streets. That's my turf. You guys can just stick to getting money here at school."

"Alright."

"If I find out that you're still selling on the streets, your next visit with me will not end well. I don't have a problem with putting you and your buddy six feet under if you disrespect me again."

All the other guys with Pistol P start laughing. I hate these bastards.

"Now, you're free to go," he says. "Don't forget what we talked about today. Go to class boy."

Chapter Fifteen

FOR THE PAST week, I've been on the straight and narrow. My pockets are really hurting now, which has me sort of tempted to start back selling at school. Derek hasn't been to school since last week. Our last face to face conversation got a little heated, but we talked on the phone a few days ago to patch things up. Even though I told Derek about my restroom encounter with Pistol P, he still refuses to stop roaming the streets to make money. All I can do at this point is just pray for him and hope that he doesn't get caught up in anything.

After shoving all my books into my locker, I stroll on down the hallway toward the front of the school. As I'm coming up on Mr. Newman's class, he's standing in his doorway with his arms folded. Monitoring the activity in the hallway is one of Mr. Newman's favorite hobbies.

"Avery!" Mr. Newman yells. "Come talk to me for a minute son."

"Okay," I say.

We go inside his classroom and I pull up a chair to his desk.

"How is everything going for you son?" he asks.

"Everything is going good these days," I say. "I can't complain."

"That's good," he says. "I wanted to let you know that you've been doing a really good job in my class."

"Thanks Mr. Newman," I say. "I try my best to stay on top of my work."

"Your grades have been impressive! You got the highest overall grade in my fourth period class."

"Wow! That's great. I knew I was doing good in here, but I didn't know I was leading the class like that."

"Yeah—you've set the tone in here for sure. How are your grades looking in your other classes?"

"I got mostly A's and a couple B's in my other classes."

"That's what's up son."

"I met with my guidance counselor not too long ago. She told me that with my grade point average, I'll be graduating in the top of my class this year."

"I'm sure your mother is very proud of you. I'm definitely proud of you son."

"She is. I promised her that I'd always stay on top of my schoolwork. I always keep my promises, especially with her."

"Have you submitted any applications for college yet?" he asks.

"I sure have," I say. "I've submitted applications to three schools. I'm just waiting for them to respond now. I've applied for financial aid too."

"I got some information I'd like to give you," he says.

Mr. Newman reaches into his desk drawer and pulls out a red folder. He hands me the folder with a big smile on his face.

"What's this Mr. Newman?" I ask.

"This is a list of college scholarships you'd qualify for," he says. "I want you to take advantage of this son. You'll be able to use any of these scholarships toward whatever school you choose to attend."

"That's what's up," I say. "Good looking out Mr. Newman!"

"No problem son," he says. "Hurry up and apply for those scholarships as soon as possible. The deadline to apply for them are coming up."

"I'm getting on top of this immediately," I say. "I'll start looking over this today when I get home."

"Good," he says. "Make it happen son."

"Thanks Mr. Newman," I say. "I'll show this to my mama too when I get home."

"You're welcome son. Tell Ms. Johnson I said hello."

"I will. See you tomorrow Mr. Newman."

"Okay. Take care son."

Once I make it outside in front of the school, I see Jessica heading toward the parking lot. I race down the stairs and manage to catch up with her right before she gets into her car.

"Hold on beautiful," I say.

"Hey Avery," she says. "How are you?"

"I'm cool," I say. "What about you?"

"I'm alright," she says. "Nothing new going on with me."

"Same here."

"I've noticed that you've been keeping your nose clean lately. I guess you've slowed down after all."

"I wasn't lying to you the last time we talked. I've just been concentrating on my schoolwork and applying for different colleges."

"I'm glad you've been doing that."

"Yeah, me too. Have you started getting ready for prom yet?"

"Boy—yes! I've been looking at a few dresses online and I might go visit some stores this weekend."

"So . . . I guess you already have a date for the prom now."

"No—not yet. No one has asked me to go with them. I'm just going solo for now."

I can't believe nobody has asked Jessica to the prom. Maybe guys are just afraid to ask her. Some people don't take rejection well. This is the perfect opportunity for me. She could turn me down if I ask her, but it's worth the try. I have nothing to lose.

Then I say, "You shouldn't go to the prom alone. Any guy would be extremely glad to have you on their arm that night. Can I take you to the prom?"

"Are you sure you want to take little ole me?" she asks, smiling from ear to ear.

"Yeah. What do you want to do?"

"I'll go with you Avery."

"Cool! It's a date then."

"I think we're going to have a really good time. I'm excited!"

"Yeah—we will. I'm excited too. I'll let you be on your way now. We can talk about all the details a little later."

"Okay. Just give me a call when you can."

"I will. Can I get a hug Jessica?"

"You sure can."

Jessica gives me a nice warm hug. Getting a hug from Jessica and securing her as my prom date has really made my day. I feel like I've hit the jackpot.

"See you later Avery," she says.

"See you later boo," I say.

Jessica gets into her car and drives away. I can't wait to tell Derek that I finally got her. I'm sure he's going to be a little jealous, but he'll be alright.

When I finally make it home from school, I'm welcomed by Derek, who's sitting on my front porch.

"What's up Derek?" I ask.

"Not much," he says. "I was just stopping by to talk to you for a minute."

"How long have you been out here on the porch?" I ask.

"Not long," he says. "I've been out here for about ten minutes. Your mama told me I could wait on you out here."

"I got some really good news to share with you my brother," I say.

"What news is that?" he asks.

"I asked Jessica to the prom today and she said that she'll go with me. That just made my day!"

"Congratulations bro. That's a big win for you right there. You're lucky to pull that off."

"What does luck have to do with it?"

"You're lucky because she would've asked me to the prom if I had been at school lately."

I laugh. I knew he'd be a little jealous.

"You're crazy Derek," I say. "I think you probably forgot to take your medicine today or you've bumped your head on something."

"Whatever dude," he says.

"Whatever my butt. Anyway, what did you want to talk about?"

"Before we get into that, I think you should go in the house and check on your mama."

"Why? What's wrong with my mama?"

"She was looking a little upset when I first got here. Maybe that's why she told me to wait on the front porch for you. Go check on her."

"Alright. I'll be back in a few minutes."

When I get inside the house, I find Mama sitting in the kitchen by herself crying.

"Why are you crying Mama?" I ask.

"Life is really kicking my butt right now son," she says. "My warehouse job is about to let me go for good. I don't know what I'm going to do."

"You've been working there for quite a while now," I say. "Why would they just let you go after all this time?"

"Business has been really slow since the holidays are now over," she says. "Management said they have to cut most of their staff."

"*That's messed up*," I say. "You've been working there way longer than most of the people they got! You should've been one of the last workers they even considered to let go."

"I know son," she says. "But my manager doesn't really like me. I don't know why because I've *never* done anything to her. When it came down to them choosing the people who were being let go, I bet she couldn't wait to pick my name. That lady is a very mean person."

"That's not fair at all! I hate they're doing you like that Mama."

"Life isn't fair son. You should know that by now. I don't know how we're going to make it. My other part-time job is only paying for groceries and household stuff we need."

"We'll figure something out Mama," I say.

"I'm trying my best to stay strong son," she says. "But it's really hard now since this is happening."

She walks over to me and hugs me tight. I embrace her and I can feel the tears running down her face. She has so much stress on her now. Seeing her like this is breaking my heart into pieces.

"I'm going to do as much as I can to help out around here Mama," I say. "Go sit down in your room and try to relax for a minute."

"I'll try," she says, wiping her face with her shirt.

"Derek is still out on the front porch," I say. "Once I finish talking to him, I'll come back in and check on you."

"Okay son," she says. "Do you have any money on you right now?"

"Yeah. I got a few dollars."

"Can you go to the store and buy me something to drink? The only thing we got in the refrigerator is water. I want something else to drink."

"I'll go get you something Mama. What kind of drink do you want?"

"You can get me some orange juice if they have it. If not, you can just bring me back a fruit punch drink."

"Say no more. I'll be back in a little bit."

After Mama goes into her room, I go back to the front porch with Derek.

"Everything is so messed up right now bro!" I say. "We *never* get ahead and I'm getting so tired of this!"

"What's wrong bro?" Derek asks.

"My mama is about to be let go from her warehouse job," I say.

"That's insane bro," Derek says. "She's been working at that warehouse for a while."

"That's the same thing I said to my mama a few minutes ago. They're doing her dirty bro."

"That's a fact. They're wrong for that. What are you going to do?"

"I'm thinking about calling my pastor to see if he can help," I say. "He hooked my mama up with that part-time job she got, so he might be able to help her get something full-time."

"That's what's up," he says. "How soon do you think he'll be able to help her find something full-time?"

"See . . . that's the thing," I say. "There's no telling how long it might be before he can find her something full-time. She needs something right now!"

"You're right about that bro," he says. "What's your next move?"

"I guess . . . it's time for me to get on my grind and get back to selling that product," I say. "I really don't have a choice at this point. If I don't, we'll be living on the streets."

"That's what I'm talking about bro! You got to handle your business to survive right now. I got your back the whole way."

"I figured you would," I say. "You've been wanting me to get back at it anyway."

"It's easy money bro," he says. "It can't get no easier than this."

"You're right about it being easy money," I say. "That easy money comes with a major risk too. I guess I'll have to take that risk right now. I can make some decent money selling to folks at school."

"We'll be alright bro," he says. "Besides the school clientele, are you going to start back selling on the streets with me too?"

BCM is my main concern when it comes to selling on the streets. Even though BCM gave us a warning not too long ago, Derek seems to not be bothered or care.

Then I say, "I'm going to mainly stick to selling at school. Every now and then, I'll do a transaction or two on the streets. I'll have to make sure none of those BCM dudes are around if I do."

"Man . . . forget those clowns," Derek says. "I'm not worried about them at all."

"Those dudes are serious Derek. I'm not going back to selling heavy on the streets like that. You can keep doing it, but I'm good."

"Okay," Derek says.

"There's one thing I want you to do for me," I say.

"I'm listening bro."

"I want you to start back coming to school on the regular basis. You've been missing a lot of days lately. Making this money is good and all, but we both need to cross that stage in May."

"I will bro. I haven't forgotten about school. I've just been trying to stack up my money this past week. I'll start back coming to school every day."

"You promise?"

"I promise bro. I really want to graduate."

"Cool. I don't want you bugging out our senior year and not graduate."

"I got this bro! And you really need to stack up your money now since you're taking Jessica to the prom. Everything has to be on point that night."

"I'll have everything covered," I say. "I can't let Jessica find out that I'm back to selling weed again. She's only letting me get back close to her because I had stopped selling for a while."

"It's going to be hard for you to keep that under wraps for long," he says.

"I know. But I'll try my best. She just doesn't know what I'm up against."

"Well—I understand. Handle your business bro."

"I will. My family is depending on me."

"Do you want to come over my house and hang out for a little bit?" he asks.

"Maybe another time," I say. "I'm about to go to the store and get my mama something to drink."

"Alright. I'll walk with you if you want me to."

"That's cool. Let's roll out."

Chapter Sixteen

THESE PAST TWO weeks have been very profitable. Every so often, I've managed to do a few transactions on my way home from school without anyone from BCM noticing. I refuse to start back selling heavy in the streets like Derek. Supplying weed smokers at school will continue to be my main concentration.

Even though money has been steadily coming in, it's quickly leaving my hands and going toward bills. Ever since Mama got laid off from her full-time job, she's had a difficult time finding something new. Until she finds another full-time job, I got to keep us afloat.

As I'm leaving out of the front door, Cameron runs up behind me and tugs on my shirt very hard. I wonder what he wants now.

"How can I help you little man?" I ask. "I got to go handle some business."

"I don't really want anything," Cameron says. "I just wanted to tell you thanks."

"Thanks for what?" I ask.

"Thanks for helping Mama take care of the house and me," Cameron says.

"It's nothing little man," I say. "I'm just doing what I can."

"I know you are big bro. Will Mama find another job soon?"

"I'm sure she will. She's been going to the library just about every day to do applications online. She'll find something Cameron."

"I hope you're right."

"We're going to be alright little man. Now, go watch some cartoons or something. Don't worry about Mama."

"I'll make me and Mama some syrup sandwiches first," Cameron says. "I know she's hungry too. I'll go watch some cartoons after I do that. Bye ugly boy."

I exit the front door and head to the neighborhood's hot wing restaurant to meet up with Derek. Once I make it to the restaurant, I buy something to drink and go sit with Derek.

"You didn't order any wings bro?" Derek asks.

"Uh . . . no," I say. "I'm really not that hungry right now. I see you got a box full of those honey gold wings. They do smell good."

"They taste even better bro," Derek says, smacking his lips. "Do you want one of these?"

"No. I'll get some wings when we get ready to leave."

"Avery . . . business has been *beautiful* these past few weeks."

"You're definitely right my friend. But all the money I've made has gone toward my house."

"Ms. Johnson still haven't found another job yet?"

"Not yet bro."

"That sucks."

"*Tell me* about it. I hope she finds one soon."

"It's hard out here for us black folks," Derek says. "It's even harder for single black mothers. Ms. Johnson is a very strong woman."

"She's been strong for a long time," I say. "She's been taking care of Cameron and I by herself since . . . forever."

"That's how it normally goes," Derek says. "Neither one of us have ever had a real father in our lives."

For all I know, my daddy could be dead, in jail, or off somewhere else starting another family. Things would probably be a little easier if he was around. At this point in my life, I don't even care where he's at right now. It's not important to me.

"Are you getting excited about prom bro?" Derek asks.

"Just a little bit," I say. "I'm not sure if I'll even have enough money to go."

"I'll let you borrow some money," he says. "You're going to the prom bro! You got one of the finest girls at school as your date. You can't let her down."

"I'm aware of that," I say. "Whatever you can let me borrow, I'll appreciate it bro."

"I'll drop some cash on you tomorrow," he says.

"I'll definitely be waiting to receive it," I say.

"And . . . I got some more good news about prom," he says."

"Inform me please."

"My cousin is going to let us borrow his car for prom. He just told me the other day that we can use it."

"Are you talking about the Chevy Tahoe with the big rims on it?"

"Yes! We're going to be riding in style that night. I can't wait!"

"Man . . . everybody is going to be scoping us out. I'm sure our dates are going to love it too."

"Exactly! We'll be the cleanest ones pulling up on prom night."

As Derek and I continue to talk about prom night, our good buddy Wayne rushes up to our table in a hurry. From the look on his face, something's wrong.

"Get up guys!" Wayne says. "Your folks are in trouble Avery!"

"What are you talking about?" I ask. "What's going on?"

"Your house just got shot up a minute ago!" Wayne says. "I heard loud screaming and yelling coming from your house after the shots stopped."

As soon as Wayne said that, an overflow of rage came over me.

"Let's get out of here!" I yell.

We all race out of the restaurant as fast as possible. All of us are running at full speed to get to my house. Derek almost gets hit by a car while running in the street.

When we finally get to my house, a few police cars and an ambulance is in front of the house. There are a ton of bullet holes across the front of the house. The front living room window is completely shattered. After a few seconds, I spot Mama standing across the street talking to one of the police officers.

"Are you alright Mama?" I ask.

"No!" she yells. "This is ridiculous."

"Did you get hurt?" I ask.

"No—I'm okay physically," she says. "The only thing that's hurt right now is my feelings. These fools shot up my house!"

"Where's Cameron Mama?"

"He's sitting in the back of the ambulance."

"Did he get . . ."

"A bullet grazed his arm, but he's okay. They almost killed me and my baby!

I run over to the ambulance to check on Cameron. The paramedics have placed a large white band aid on his left arm.

"How are you feeling little man?" I ask.

"I'm good Avery," Cameron says. "I'm a certified gangster now. I took a bullet and I'm still alive."

"I'm glad you didn't get hurt that bad," I say. "I'm sorry this happened to you Cameron."

"Is Mama still talking to the police?" he asks.

"Yeah," I say. "They're writing up a report and doing their investigation. Where were you when this happened?"

"I was in the living room. Mama and I were watching television when they started shooting at the house. It was a lot of guns shooting at one time."

"I know somebody around here saw something," I say. "I wonder who did this."

"Maybe they shot up our house by accident," he says. "I think they had the wrong house Avery."

Derek walks over to us.

"I don't know who'd be stupid enough to shoot up your house," Derek says. "Thank God that your mama and little brother are okay."

"I don't have beef with anybody right now," I say. "Neither does my mama or little brother."

"I just *told* you Avery that they had the wrong house," Cameron says. "We don't do nothing to nobody around here."

"Your brother could be right Avery," Derek says. "Stuff like that does happen every so often."

"I don't know," I say. "Hopefully, the police will find out who did this."

"That's if they can get any witnesses to step up and talk," Derek says.

"Hang tight with the paramedics Cameron," I say. "I'll be back in a few minutes. Come on Derek."

Derek and I walk over to Wayne. He's sitting on the curb by a police car.

"Did you see anything Wayne when this went down?" I ask.

"No," Wayne says. "Sorry young blood. I was right around the corner from your house when I heard the shots going off."

"Dang!" I say.

"I did hear a car burning rubber and take off really fast," Wayne says. "By the time I got closer to your house, nobody was around. That's when I heard your folks screaming from the house. The old lady across the street from your house called the police."

As we're standing there talking, an unfamiliar guy off the street walks right up to us. He's holding something in his hand.

"I don't mean to bother you all," the guy says. "I came to bring you something Avery."

"Who are you?" I ask. "And how do you know my name?"

"I swear I don't want any trouble," the guy says. "I was just paid to bring you a message. The man that paid me told me your name."

"What man?" I ask.

"I don't know his name," the guy says. "He's a local drug dealer. Here's the note he wanted me to give you."

The guy hands me the note and walks away. I open the note and it reads: I told you to stop selling in my hood without my permission. Now look at the mess you created. This is what happens when you disrespect me. If I hear that you are selling on my turf again, you won't make it to see your next birthday. - Pistol P

I can't believe this dude had the audacity to come for my precious family. I could've lost my mama and little brother over this.

"What does the note say?" Derek asks.

"It's from that fool Pistol P," I say. "He's the one that did this bro!"

"That bastard is going to pay for this!" Derek says. "He didn't have to do that."

"That's messed up young blood," Wayne says. "He didn't have to be a punk like that."

"What are we going to do Avery?" Derek asks. "We got to do something about this."

"I don't know Derek," I say. "This dude is dangerous. As bad as I want to do something, I don't think I should."

"You can't be serious!" Derek says.

"I'm not going to retaliate bro. And I'm done with selling weed for now on."

"Bro . . . you're crazy," Derek says. "This dude just shot up your house with your family in it! How can you just let that slide?"

"Pistol P got plenty of goons bro," I say. "BCM is at least fifteen men strong. There's no way we could even take them on like that."

"He got a point Derek," Wayne says. "Plus, those dudes aren't scared at all to use guns. Just look at what they did today."

"This is crazy," Derek says. "I don't care about how many goons Pistol P got. He can be touched just like anybody else on the street."

"He'll be hard to get to Derek," I say. "You know that. I'm just done with everything for now on. If I hadn't been still selling weed on the streets, none of this would've happened."

"Wayne . . . please talk some sense into this guy," Derek says.

"This whole situation is tragic Avery," Wayne says. "I hear what you and Derek are saying. Too bad you've decided to stop selling. This is messing up our business together, but I feel where you're coming from young blood."

"I'm glad you understand Wayne," I say. "To be honest, if none of us don't stop selling on the streets, we all could end up dead."

"Well—I'm not stopping!" Derek says. "Forget Pistol P! If he *ever* tries to come for me, I'm laying that dude down. I'm not playing."

"I don't care what you do Derek," I say. "I'm out the game bro. You can have it."

"I have to go guys," Wayne says. "I got some business to handle. I'll see you all later. Take care of yourself Avery. Stay strong young blood."

"I will."

Wayne gives Derek and I a quick fist bump and walks away. A few seconds later, my phone starts ringing. It's Jessica calling.

"Hey Jessica," I say.

"Hey Avery," she says. "Are you and your family okay? One of my friends that stay in your neighborhood just called and told me about what happened."

"I'm alright," I say. "I wasn't at home when my house got shot up, but my folks were there. They're doing okay though."

"That's really good to hear," she says. "I was a little worried for a minute."

"We're good," I say. "Thanks for calling and checking up on us."

"No problem," she says. "I'm sorry that happened to you all. These people in this city are crazy."

"Yeah—they surely are," I say.

"There's something else I wanted to tell you too."

"What's that?"

"I've changed my mind about going to the prom with you Avery. I'm going by myself."

"Uh, okay. What made you change your mind about going with me?"

"I decided not to go with you because you got a lot going on right now. I also found out that you've started back selling weed again around school. I really thought you were done with that Avery."

"I thought I was too Jessica. But I really needed to make some money."

"Your house got shot up because you've gotten caught up in some street mess."

"Jessica—let me explain to you what . . ."

"I can't be involved with you under these circumstances Avery. I told you a long time ago that I don't want to get mixed up in *any* drama you got going on. I'm sorry."

"You don't understand what I'm going through Jessica! I don't have it *made* like you. You're not in my shoes. You don't have to deal with the things I deal with on a regular basis."

"I wish the best for you Avery. I really hate to change things up like this, but I can't do it. I just wanted to check on you and tell you that. Goodbye Avery."

Jessica hangs up the phone. My feelings are beyond hurt now. I don't think Jessica will ever have anything else to do with me. Everything that happened today is my fault, but all I've been trying to do is help my family survive these hard times we're having. I have too much to deal with on the regular basis. I wish life was a little easier for me. Today is by far the worst day of my life.

Chapter Seventeen

FOR THE PAST three nights, our church member Ms. Brown has let Mama and Cameron spend the night at her house. After what happened to our house the other day, Mama felt more comfortable if we stayed somewhere else for a while. Plus, there are many repairs that need to be made to our house. Pastor Wright has been generous enough to let me stay at his house for the time being. Also, he took it upon himself to make sure all the repairs get done to our house. He's gathered a team of men and they've been working on the front of our house since the day after the shooting.

After I take a shower and put on my clothes, I head into the kitchen to eat breakfast with Pastor Wright. All the food he's cooked this morning looks delicious. He's cooked bacon, eggs, pancakes, hash browns, and oatmeal. I had no idea he could cook like this.

"Make yourself a plate son," Pastor Wright says, while hanging up his apron. "You can get as much as you want."

"Okay," I say. "Thanks Pastor."

"What do you want to drink?" he asks.

"What do you have?"

"I got some orange juice, apple juice, and of course water."

"I'll take some orange juice."

"Good choice son. I guess I'll have that too."

Pastor Wright grabs the orange juice from the refrigerator and pours both of us a tall glass. Once we sit down at the kitchen table, Pastor Wright prays over the food and we begin to dig in.

"You've been mighty quiet these past few days son," he says. "You hardly ever come out of the guest bedroom. Are you alright?"

"Yeah, I'm okay," I say. "I've just been relaxing."

"Well—that's about to change today," he says. "I'm putting you to work. You're going over to the house with me in a little bit to help with the repairs. We're just about done with everything."

"That's no problem," I say. "I don't mind helping out with the repairs."

"I knew you wouldn't mind helping out. After all, your continuous activity on the streets is probably the main reason why this happened in the first place."

My mouth drops. I can already tell where this conversation is going.

"You're right Pastor," I say. "This whole thing is completely my fault. I'll take ownership of that. I've still been out there hustling on the streets like an idiot."

"Obviously, you didn't take my advice the last time we talked about this," he says. "I'm very disappointed in you right now."

"I'm sorry, sir," I say. "I know I should've taken your advice. I've screwed up big time."

"I hope that all of this has taught you a valuable lesson now. Your mother and little brother could've died that day son."

"I'm completely done with trying to get money like that. I'm not messing with that crap anymore."

"That's good son. God wasn't pleased with what you were doing out there. This neighborhood has already been deteriorating because of drugs and you were adding to the problem."

"When I first started doing it, I wasn't thinking about that. I am now since you brought it to my attention. My main motive was to just make some easy money to help out at home."

"That so-called *easy* money comes with consequences son. For the most part, you'll eventually end up hurt, in jail, or in a casket."

"I know Pastor."

"I want you to start building a better relationship with God Avery. I want you to come to church more often too. You need to get more into the word."

"I will Pastor Wright," I say. "I really want to do right and live right on a consistent basis."

"I know that you and your family have had some problems," he says. "But you have to make better decisions son and have faith in God. God will fight your battles for you when you trust him and hand everything over to him."

"I hear you Pastor."

Pastor Wright always has the right advice to give. I really need to get my life back on track. I can't have anything else happen to my family because of my actions and bad decisions.

"That job I offered you a while ago is still open son," he says.

"Are you talking about the part-time cleaning job for the church?" I ask.

"Yeah, that's the one," he says.

"I'll go ahead and take it," I say. "I can do that for you Pastor."

"Okay," he says. "The job is all yours."

"What days would you need me to work?" I ask.

"I just need you every Monday and Thursday evening for about four hours."

"Is that all?"

"That's all son. It doesn't take much to maintain the church. That's all the hours needed to get the job done."

"Okay. I appreciate the opportunity."

"No problem son."

"I just want you to know that I'll still be applying for other jobs in the meantime too Pastor."

"I know you will son. I totally understand. I'm just trying to help you out the best way I can. Don't lose focus of staying on top of your schoolwork. You'll be graduating this year."

"I'm on it," I say.

"Make sure you keep it that way."

I do have some homework I need to be finishing up. I'll get it done later today.

"I have a question I want to ask you Pastor," I say.

"What is it son?" he asks.

"Are you going to tell my mama that I was selling weed and I'm the reason why our house got shot up?" I ask.

"No," he says. "I'll leave it up to you to decide if you want to tell her or not. I'm not getting into that."

"Thanks Pastor," I say.

"Don't thank me son," he says. "You better just take my advice and get your act together like you said you would. I'll contact the police and turn you in *myself* if I see you out there selling drugs. Handle your business and get yourself together son."

"I am," I say.

"I don't want to see you end up in jail or dead because of selling drugs," he says. "I want to see you draw closer to God and live a more righteous lifestyle."

"I'll get my act together," I say. "I promise you that. I got to be a better role model for my little brother. He looks up to me."

"I bet he does," he says. "He's watching everything you do."

"I know."

"I bet he's a hand full for Ms. Johnson too. Most boys are at that age."

"He's not *that* bad, but he does have his moments."

"Let me go freshen up and grab my car keys," he says. "We'll be stopping by the hardware store before we go to your house."

"Cool," I say.

"Put your dishes in the sink and wait for me in the living room," he says.

"Will do."

After Pastor Wright gets himself together, we get into his truck and head down to the hardware store. When we get there, he buys some nails and paint for the front porch. We load everything onto his truck and head on to my house.

Once we make it to my house, I notice that the men working on the house have pretty much finished the repairs. Everything looks good. The only thing left to do is to add paint to the front porch. Pastor Wright gives me a bucket of paint and shows me the section of the porch he wants me to work on.

In just a couple of hours, everything is all done. I give all the men a handshake and thank them for helping with the house. From listening to them talk when working on the house, I discovered that all of them are police officers. When not in uniform, they all do maintenance work as a side hustle.

After thanking them, they all load up their tools onto their trucks and go their separate ways. Pastor Wright and I go inside the house to get something to drink from the kitchen.

"Everything turned out just fine son," Pastor Wright says.

"It sure did," I say. "Thanks again for helping us out Pastor. I don't know what we'd do without you."

"You're welcome son," he says. "God has blessed me in so many ways. I just try to bless others whenever I can. Plus, I must take care of all my members."

"And you do that well," I say.

"Thanks son," he says, stroking his beard.

"Do you want some more water?" I ask.

"No—I'm good son," he says. "You can stay at home now. The front door is good and everything else is fixed."

"That's what's up," I say. "Have you told my mama that everything is good now?"

"I called her earlier and told her we were just about done with the house," he says. "When I get to my truck, I'll call her again and let her know she can come home now."

"Okay."

"Let me get out of here son. It's been real. I'll see you later."

"See you later. Take care Pastor."

Chapter Eighteen

I WAKE UP to my bedroom door being slammed extremely hard. I look over towards the door and its Mama. I know this is not good. Before I can fully sit up, she rushes over to my bed and starts slapping and punching me repeatedly.

"You got me messed up boy!" she yells. "Get your trifling butt up!"

"Stop hitting me Mama!" I say, struggling to get away from her.

"I can't believe you Avery!" she yells. "You really did it this time!"

After slapping and punching me several times, she grabs me by the collar of my shirt and yanks me completely out of the bed onto the floor.

"What's going on Mama?" I ask.

"It's your fault that my house got shot up last week!" she yells. "You've been out here selling weed on the streets!"

"Can I just. . ."

"Someone from the police station called me this morning to give me an update on the shooting investigation. After questioning people around the neighborhood, they said just about *everybody* they talked to said you've been selling weed in the neighborhood recently."

With me being guilty and telling her so many lies lately, I owe Mama the truth now. It's time for me to take responsibility like a man.

"I'm sorry Mama," I say. "It's true, but I stopped selling weed now. I'm really sorry for everything I've done."

"Get up off the floor," she says.

I get up from the floor and sit on my bed.

"Why have you been selling weed Avery?" she asks.

"I only started selling a little weed to make some money Mama," I say.

"I figured something had to be going on for that to happen to us," she says. "I just couldn't put my finger on it. Houses normally get shot up when people in the house got some mess going on in the streets. You almost got us killed Avery!"

"I'm so sorry Mama. I didn't mean for that to happen. I chose to sell weed because I couldn't find a job and we needed the money really bad."

"I don't want to hear that," she says. "As bad as you thought we needed the money, you still shouldn't have done it."

"I didn't want us to ever get put out the house or go without food," I say. "There was even a time when we almost got our utilities cut off."

"I'm the parent Avery!" she says. "You just let me be concerned about that."

"I can't help but to be concerned about it too Mama. It affects all of us. I don't want us to ever be homeless or go without."

"That's not going to happen boy!"

"I know it's your responsibility to take care of us and the house, but you've been struggling to do that on your own. You haven't even found another full-time job yet."

"I'll get something soon. God will always make sure we get taken care of, even during the hard and difficult times we face son."

With the way things were going before I started hustling, it never seemed like our problems were going to get better. I had to make something happen and it worked for a while.

Then Mama says, "You always got to have faith son. Our faith may sometimes get a little shaky when things get rough, but we must always believe that God got us."

"I hear you," I say.

"I want you to hear this too," she says. "If I find out you're still involved with selling that mess from here on out, I'm putting you out of my house. Do you understand me?"

"Yes, ma'am," I say. "I promise I'm done with that for good."

"You better be," she says. "I won't tolerate any children of mine selling drugs while living under my roof."

"I understand Mama."

"You got a bright future Avery. I never want to see you mess that up. You need to go to college and make something of yourself. Then, you won't have to live and struggle like I do son."

"I will Mama. I'll take care of business."

"Good. Now, get up and get yourself together."

Mama walks out of my room and closes the door behind her. I got to get back on her good side. After everything I've done, I got to do right for now on to gain back her trust.

After taking a shower and getting dressed, I head to the living room to check the mail before I leave the house. Once I make my way out of the front door, I'm met by Mama on the porch.

"Where are you going Avery?" she asks.

"I'm heading out to go see about a few jobs today," I say. "Pastor Wright gave me a job cleaning up at the church twice a week, but I won't be able to get that many hours."

"Are all these jobs you're going to see about legit and legal?" she asks, rolling her neck.

"Yes, ma'am," I say. "I'm stopping by the supermarket first. I heard they're hiring right now."

"Okay," she says. "Let me know if they have any full-time positions open."

"I will."

"And bring me back a bag of barbeque potato chips. Your brother keeps finding my chips when I hide them. He eats them all up with his greedy self."

"Okay."

After a nice long stroll through the neighborhood, I finally make it to the supermarket. Once I get inside, I spot someone who looks like one of the managers for the store. The man has a walkie talkie on his hip and he's giving orders to some of the other workers in the front of the store. I approach him and he greets me with a smile.

"Are you the head store manager?" I ask.

"I sure am," he says. "My name is Rick. How can I help you today?"

"My name is Avery," I say. "I wanted to see about becoming a part-time grocery stocker. Do you all still need people for that position?"

"Yes—we still need grocery stockers," he says. "What is your current availability?"

"I can work on evenings and nights," I say. "I'm still in high school, but I'll be graduating this year. I can work anytime on the weekends too."

"I may be able to use you," he says. "You'll have to go online and fill out an application on our website."

"I can do that today," I say.

"Okay. Give me your contact information. After I pull your application and review it, I'll give you a call to set up an interview."

"Do you have a pen I can use Rick?"

"Sure."

Rick gives me a black ink pen. I write down my name and phone number on the back of an old receipt from my wallet and hand it to Rick.

"Thanks," he says. "I'll be giving you a call soon Avery."

"I'll be looking forward to it," I say. "Here's your pen back too."

I hand Rick his pen.

"Thanks," he says. "I'll need that later."

"I got one more question," I say.

"Go for it," he says.

"Do you have any full-time positions open? My mama is looking for a full-time job. I think she has experience working in a grocery store."

"We do. Tell her to fill out an application online when she gets a chance."

"Alright. Thanks."

"You're welcome. Take care."

As I'm walking out of the supermarket, I cross paths with my homeboy Derek.

"What's going on bro?" I ask, dapping up Derek.

"Just chilling and making moves as usual," Derek says. "What are you doing up here?"

"I'm trying to get a job up here," I say. "They're hiring right now."

"Good luck with that," Derek says. "I've been missing you running the streets with me bro. It's been different without you."

"I bet it has," I say. "I can't get back into doing that bro. You need to be careful while you're out there on the streets."

"I am," Derek says. "I always make sure I keep that heat on me, except for today. I left it at home this morning by accident. I'm going back to get it in a little while."

"How is Wayne doing?" I ask.

"He's doing alright. He asked about you the other day. He said he tried to call you not too long ago, but your phone was off."

"It's been off for a couple days now. I'll be putting some more minutes on it soon."

"Okay. What have you been doing lately for money?"

"I'm broke right now. My pastor just gave me a part-time gig cleaning the church two days a week. I start working this week. I'll get my first check next week."

"If you need to borrow some money until then, just say the word and I'll help you out."

"Okay—will do."

"Are you still going to be working at the church too once you find another job?"

"I don't think so. I'll probably have to let the cleaning job go. My pastor already knows I'm trying to find something else that would give me more days and hours."

"I figured that," Derek says. "What are you about to do now?"

"I was about to go check and see if the shoe store down the street is hiring," I say. "I might just stop by there tomorrow. I'm getting hungry now. I need to find something to eat."

"Come kick it with me at my house," Derek says. "You can get something to eat there."

"Alright. Let's do it."

Derek and I begin walking to his house. After walking for about ten minutes, we get approached by a random guy with a big afro.

"Hello fellas," the guy says. "Anyone of you got that good weed for sale?"

"I got you covered," Derek says. "How much are you looking to buy?"

"What can I get for ten dollars?" the guy asks.

"*Hold on*," I say. "Derek, can you not do that right now? Let him get some weed from somewhere else."

"Come on bro," Derek says. "Let me make this quick transaction. It'll only take a few seconds."

"Alright bro," I say. "But don't do this around me anymore."

"You're doing the most," Derek says. "But I'll respect your wishes bro."

As Derek and the guy are making their exchange, I spot two men down the street watching us. They both look like they could be BCM members. Within a matter of seconds, the two men start jogging in our direction while pulling guns from their waistband.

"Let's go Derek!" I say, tapping him on the arm. "Two BCM dudes are coming our way with guns!"

"Where?" Derek asks.

Then suddenly, two gunshots go off. The bullets strike a car that's right next to us, shattering one of its windows. The guy Derek was selling weed to takes off running and hollering.

"Oh snap!" Derek yells. "Let's go bro!"

Derek and I take off running as fast as we can. The two BCM shooters start chasing us. After a short distance, Derek and I go off into a nearby alley on the side of a convenience store. As we're still running, I look back and see the two guys hot on our trail. I'm keeping a good pace, but Derek is starting to slowly fall behind. He's barely keeping up with me.

"Keep up bro!" I yell. "We can lose them up ahead when we get to this street."

"I'm right behind you track star!" Derek says. "I'm good bro."

Once we're out of the alley, we both dodge a few cars and make it across the busy street. Then, we take off between two large buildings. Derek is still struggling to keep pace with me while we're navigating between the buildings. After a few seconds, we turn a corner and I see a tall fence about thirty yards ahead of us.

"Let's get over that fence!" I yell.

I make it to the fence first. I jump as high as I can and try to catch a good grip toward the top of the fence. With my good efforts, I manage to get a nice grip very close to the top of the fence. I pull myself up and make it over to the other side. After I jump down and continue to run, I look back for a second and I see Derek struggling to get over the fence. I stop running immediately to let him catch up.

"Hurry up bro!" I yell.

"I'm trying!" Derek yells. "This fence is high!"

As Derek is climbing up the fence, the two BCM guys come around the corner.

"Come on Derek!" I yell.

Right when Derek is making it to the top of the fence, a couple gunshots go off. Derek is struck in the back by the bullets and he falls off the fence.

"No!" I yell.

The two BCM guys walk up to Derek while he's on the ground and shoots him two more times at close range. I can't believe what I'm witnessing. The two guys then take off running in the opposite direction and never look back. I run and leap back over the tall fence as quickly as I can. As I grab Derek, he's gasping for air and is bleeding heavily.

"Hold on bro!" I say. "I can't lose you!"

"I don't want to die Avery," Derek says with tears running down his face.

"Help!" I yell out. "We need help!"

"I love you Avery," Derek says.

"Hold on!" I say. "Let me call 911."

As I'm feeling around in Derek's pocket to find his cell phone, he stops breathing. It's too late. He's no longer moving. His blood is all over me. I can't believe that my best friend is dead.

Chapter Nineteen

MY BEST FRIEND is gone forever. I don't know what to do with all this pain and anger built up inside of me. During the funeral last week, I couldn't even pull myself together to view Derek's body before they closed the casket. Derek's mother is really taking his death hard. Derek was her only child. As I lay here in bed, I can't help but to think about how I should get revenge for my friend. He would've done the same thing for me if those bastards had taken me out like that.

The other day, Wayne did inform me that the entire BCM gang was having a mandatory meeting today around two o'clock. That would be the perfect opportunity for me to take out Pistol P and get revenge. BCM would be nothing without their so-called fearless leader. As a matter of fact, Derek did give me that rifle with the scope on it for Christmas. It should be stashed right under the house where I left it. Taking out Pistol P is the only way I can get rid of all this pain. He deserves it anyway. That fool almost killed my family too. I got to do this today.

After putting on my clothes and shoes, I go to the kitchen and gulp down a cold glass of water. When I make it into the living room, Mama stops me just before I can get to the front door. I really didn't want her to see me leaving the house.

"How are you doing son?" she asks.

"I've had better days," I say. "I've just been taking it one day at a time."

"Derek's death has been hard for all of us," she says. "I know how close both of you were. I really hate he had to leave this earth like that."

"I hate it too Mama," I say. "He died right before I was able to call 911 that day."

"I know that had to be very traumatizing and scary for you son," she says.

"It really was Mama. I've been having a hard time sleeping at night for the past week. All I've been thinking about is Derek dying in my arms that day."

"I thought I heard you up late the other night."

"Yeah. I got up and cleaned the whole kitchen when I couldn't sleep the other night. I'm a little tired now, but I'll be alright."

"I hope you get some rest soon. Have you tried to talk to Pastor Wright? He might be able to help you deal with this a little better."

"I haven't talked to him since the funeral. I thought about reaching out to him the other day to talk."

"You need to do that son. I think you could *really* use his help right about now."

With what I have planned on my agenda today, Pastor Wright is the last person I want to talk to right now. He wouldn't be pleased with what I'm about to do, but it must be done. I've tried praying every day since Derek died, but all this pain and anger won't go away.

Then I say, "I'll reach out to Pastor later."

"Okay," she says. "Make sure you do that. I got a few sleep aid pills if you want to take one tonight."

"Where are they?" I ask.

"I keep them in my room," she says. "Just let me know later if you want one for tonight."

"Okay Mama," I say. "I'm about to go out for a little bit. I'll be back soon."

"You be careful son," she says.

"I will Mama."

After Mama gives me a big hug and kiss on the cheek, I leave out of the front door. I make my way to the side of the house and crawl through a small opening to find the rifle. It's exactly where I left it. I rip off the garbage bag from the guitar case and open it quickly. The rifle is still in very good condition. Smart move by Derek to give me the rifle in this guitar case.

Within twenty minutes, I make it close to where BCM is meeting up today. They're having their mandatory meeting right by the neighborhood park. From a distance, I can see a few of them starting to arrive. Out of nowhere, Wayne walks up and startles me.

"I *knew* you'd be down for this young blood," Wayne says.

"You scared the crap out of me!" I say.

"My bad," Wayne says. "I see you got what you need to get the job done today. Are you ready to do this?"

"I think I am," I say.

"Cool," Wayne says. "Check this out young blood. There's a building right across the street that'll help you handle your business today."

Wayne points out the building to me. It's an old abandoned building that's been empty for many years. I can't even remember what it was used for in the past.

"On the side of the building, there's a fire escape that leads all the way to the top of the roof," Wayne says. "Just lay low up there and handle your business. You'll be able to get a clear shot from up there."

"Okay," I say.

"I'll be looking out for you down here on the ground young blood."

I make my way to the side of the building. As I'm going up the fire escape, I'm starting to get even more nervous. My heart is beating fast and my hands are getting sweaty. I was just fine on my way here. I was so convinced that I could go through with this whole thing today. I didn't think I'd begin to feel like this right now.

When I finally make it to the top of the roof, I find a nice area where I'm able to see everything that's going on down below by the park. Within a matter of seconds, I spot Pistol P arriving to the park. The meeting should be starting very soon. Even though my nerves are shot right now, I must go through with this. Pistol P is destroying my life and this neighborhood. If I don't stop him now, things are bound to get worse. I got to do this for Derek.

I open the guitar case and pull out the rifle. Then, I begin loading the bullets and making sure the rifle is good to go. Suddenly, my phone starts vibrating. It's Pastor Wright calling. Out of all the time in the day, he chooses to call me right now. I let his call go to voicemail, but he starts calling me again.

"What's going on Pastor Wright?" I ask.

"I'm glad you picked up son," he says. "I want to talk to you for a moment. Give me a quick minute or two of your time."

"Uh . . . okay," I say. "I can do that for you."

"Thanks son," he says. "I know your friend's death has been a little hard on you."

"Yeah," I say. "I've been trying to deal with it the best way I can."

"I hear you," he says. "As your pastor and friend, I just want to reassure you that things will get better for you in due time."

"I really don't see how things will get better soon," I say. "My best friend is gone forever. He didn't deserve to die like that. They shot him right in front of me."

"I know you're hurting right now son, but I promise you it'll get better. You're not in this alone. I'm here to help you get through this tough time."

"Those bastards killed my best friend!" I say. "They're still on the loose and somebody needs to do something! What about them?"

"I'm confident that they'll eventually get caught."

"You really can't be sure of that! A lot of people have been killed in this neighborhood and their killers were never caught. I don't want that for Derek. I want the people who . . ."

"*Listen* son. Everything is going to work out."

Tears begin to run down my face.

Then Pastor Wright says, "I want you to trust me on this. More importantly, I want you to trust God. He doesn't fail his people son."

"I just want justice for my friend," I say. "Somebody has to do something."

"God will take care of that son," he says. "In the meantime, I don't want you worrying about if the police can catch those guys who killed Derek. Also, I don't want you trying to take matters into your own hands and end up doing something you'll regret later."

I almost feel like Pastor Wright can see exactly what I'm doing right now. Maybe this is God using him to intervene in this situation. There's no telling what the future will hold for me if I pull the trigger on this rifle and kill Pistol P today. Plus, I could be permanently punching my ticket to hell if I successfully go through with this. I should listen to Pastor Wright. I can't let my emotions get the best of me.

Then I say, "I hear you loud and clear Pastor. I really was thinking about doing something that wouldn't have been wise, but I'm not going to do it. I'm going to trust you on this one."

"That's what I want to hear son," he says. "Everything is in God's hands. Is there anything else you want to talk about?"

"No—I'm good," I say. "I'm really glad you called me. I feel a little better now since we've talked."

"I'll always look out for you when I can son," he says. "I want to see you do good in life. I'm here for you."

"That's good to know," I say. "I have to go now. It's really been a pleasure talking to you. We'll talk again soon."

"Okay son. Take care and God bless you."

I really needed that phone conversation. Killing Pistol P isn't worth it. Pistol P and those guys that killed Derek will get what's coming to them.

As I'm putting the rifle back into the guitar case, I suddenly hear a bunch of police sirens going off and tires screeching. I look over down by the park and there's a huge swarm of police vehicles surrounding BCM. I've never seen so many police cars and trucks in my entire life. Officers are jumping out in every direction with their weapons and police dogs. All the BCM gang members are surrendering with no hesitation at all, including Pistol P. I guess the police had this planned out today.

I quickly make my way off the roof and back to the side of the building. I toss the rifle into a nearby dumpster. When I get around to the front of the building, I'm met by Wayne.

"Did you see that young blood?" Wayne asks.

"Yeah—I did," I say. "The police came down *hard* on them boys."

"I was down here waiting a long time for you to take that shot," he says. "What happened?"

"I changed my mind about doing it," I say. "I couldn't do it."

"Well—it's probably good you didn't do it," he says. "I didn't know the police would be hot out here like that."

"They got that whole area by the park on lock down right now," I say.

"They're everywhere!" he says. "They just put the clamps on the whole BCM click. They all surrendered with the quickness. Let's go scope it out and get a closer look."

"Okay."

Wayne and I make it over to the area within seconds. By now, the police have closed off the whole scene with yellow tape. As no surprise, other people in the neighborhood that were close by have ran over to see what's going on.

From the looks of things, this is a major bust for the police. Pistol P and all the other gang members are being loaded into the back of a big police truck. Some of the police officers on the scene are packing up duffle bags with drugs and guns, which I assume they confiscated from the BCM members during the bust. These dudes are all going away for a long time. They've gotten away with a lot of stuff, but this one is going to stick for sure. I'm glad I listened to Pastor Wright and never pulled that trigger. I guess God is starting to work and change things for the better around here.

Chapter Twenty

TODAY IS THE day I've been waiting for all year long. I'm finally graduating from high school. I stayed on top of my schoolwork and have reached that sweet finish line. As the school principle is making the closing graduation speech, all I can think about is everything that's happened within this past year. I nearly lost my mama and little brother when our house got shot up. Even more heartbreaking, I lost my best friend right before my eyes. I really wish Derek was still here.

As the graduation ceremony ends, I find Mama and Cameron among the crowd of people. Mama greets me with a big hug and kiss on the cheek.

"I'm so proud of you son," Mama says.

"Thanks Mama," I say. "I finally did it!"

"I'm proud of you too big bro," Cameron says.

"Thanks Cameron."

"That's a cool cap and gown you have," Cameron says. "I can't wait until it's time for me to graduate from high school."

"You still got a long way to go little man," I say. "But you'll be taking that same walk one day for sure."

"I know," Cameron says. "I'll be graduating in the top of my class just like you."

"You sure will baby boy," Mama says. "Both of my boys are extremely smart."

"We got it from you Mama," I say.

"I need to find somebody to take a picture of us," Mama says. "I'll ask one of these parents out here in a minute to take a picture of us."

Out of nowhere, Pastor Wright walks up to us. I didn't know he was coming to the graduation.

"Hello good people," Pastor Wright says.

"Hey Pastor Wright," Mama says. "It's good to see you."

Mama and I both give Pastor Wright a hug.

"How are you doing Pastor Wright?" I ask.

"I'm doing just fine son," he says. "Congratulations on graduating today."

"Thanks. I'm surprised to see you here."

"You know I couldn't miss your big day son," he says. "This is a *major* accomplishment for you."

"Yeah—it is," I say. "I really appreciate you coming out to see me today."

"It's my pleasure," he says. "You're really coming into your own as a fine young man."

"Much of that is because of you," I say. "You've been a great mentor to me."

"Thanks son," he says. "Your mother gets more credit than anyone for your growth."

Mama smiles and blushes.

Then Pastor Wright says, "You've done a great job with both of these young men Ms. Johnson."

"Thanks Pastor," she says. "It hasn't been easy doing it alone."

"I know Ms. Johnson," he says. "You're a really strong woman and both of your sons are blessed to have you as a mother. Just continue to keep doing what you've been doing. It's working."

"I will," she says. "I'm going to *really* miss Avery when he goes off to college."

"I'll be missing you too Mama," I say. "But I'll be back home during my breaks and the holidays."

"I know son," she says.

Mama leans over and gives me another kiss on the cheek. I hope she's not leaving lipstick on my face.

"How are you liking the new job so far Ms. Johnson?" Pastor Wright asks.

"It's going really good," she says. "I thank Avery for telling me about the job."

Mama and I both got hired at the neighborhood supermarket about two weeks ago. She was hired as a full-time cashier and I've been working part-time as a grocery stocker.

Then Pastor Wright says, "That's good to hear Ms. Johnson. I'm glad it's working out for you."

"Me too," she says. "This new job was definitely a blessing from God. I have less stress now when it comes to figuring out how I'm going to take care of my home and my boys."

"Are you still working that other part-time job too?" Pastor Wright asks.

"Yeah—I am," she says. "But I've cut back my hours at the call center. They know I have a full-time job now. I hope they'll be able to continue to work with my new availability. I still want to hang on to them."

"I can imagine that joggling both of those jobs have you really tired Ms. Johnson," he says.

"They do," she says. "Some days I'm drained, but I don't complain about it. I'm just thankful that I can earn more money now."

"I hear you," he says.

"Can you take a picture of me and the boys Pastor?" she asks.

"I sure can."

"You can take the picture with my phone Pastor," I say.

"Okay."

I hand Pastor Wright my cell phone. Mama and I take a picture together first. Then, Cameron squeezes between both of us for the family photo. When we're done taking pictures and are about to leave, Jessica walks up to us. She's looking good as usual.

"Hey you," Jessica says.

"Hey Jessica," I say.

"I wanted to come and tell you congratulations," Jessica says.

"Thanks," I say. "Same to you too. We made it!"

"We sure did!" Jessica says. "Is this your family?"

"Yeah," I say. "These are my favorite people. This is my mama Ms. Sophia Johnson."

"It's nice to meet you, ma'am," Jessica says.

"Nice to meet you too Jessica," Mama says.

They both shake hands.

"You're a very pretty young lady," Mama says.

"Thank you," Jessica says.

I'm sure Mama will be asking me a ton of questions later about Jessica.

"And this is my little brother Cameron," I say.

"Hey Cameron," Jessica says.

"Hello," Cameron says.

I place my hand on Pastor Wright's shoulder.

"This man right here is like family too Jessica," I say. "This is my mentor and good friend Pastor Wright."

"It's nice to meet you Jessica," Pastor Wright says, extending his arm out to shake her hand.

"It's a pleasure to meet you too," Jessica says. "That's a very nice suit you have on."

"Thanks," Pastor Wright says. "I try my best to stay fresh, as you youngsters would say."

Jessica laughs. Pastor Wright can be a little corny at times.

"What are you about to do now Avery?" Jessica asks.

"We're about to go hit up somebody's restaurant to eat," I say.

"Okay, cool. Can we talk privately for a minute before you go?"

"Yeah. We can talk for . . ."

"We'll let you kids talk by yourselves for a few minutes," Mama says.

"I won't hold him long Ms. Johnson," Jessica says. "I promise."

"Okay," Mama says. "I need to use the restroom anyway. Cameron and I will be back in a few minutes."

"Mama, can I stay here with Avery and Jessica?" Cameron asks.

"No. You're coming with me boy."

"I'll be in my car waiting on you all," Pastor Wright says. "Take your time. I'll follow you all to whatever restaurant you decide to go to Ms. Johnson."

"Okay Pastor," Mama says. "We'll be out shortly."

Pastor Wright heads to the parking lot while Cameron slowly trails Mama to the restroom.

"I never got a chance to reach out to you when Derek died," Jessica says. "I know you both were close like brothers."

"Yeah—we were," I say. "That was really messed up what happened to him. I wish he was here to experience graduation with us today. He'll be truly missed."

"You're right," she says. "A lot of people had love for Derek. I know his death is probably still hard for you to deal with right now."

"It's gotten a little better recently," I say. "At first, it was really hard to deal with. My pastor and mama have done a good job with helping me through it."

"That's good," she says.

"How'd the prom turn out?" I ask.

"It was nice," she says.

"After what happened to Derek, I didn't even have the energy to go. Derek and I was supposed to be riding out together in style that night."

"That's understandable. I didn't take a date to the prom. I just tagged along with a couple of my friends that didn't have dates either."

"I totally understood why you declined on me for the prom," I say. "You had every right to do so. I had started back hustling and got into some mess."

"Yeah—you did."

"I should've listened to you when you first told me to stop selling weed," I say. "I could be gone like Derek, but I guess God spared me and gave me another chance to get it right."

"Well—it's all in the past now Avery. From this point on, you have a chance to live right and do what's best for yourself."

"I agree. College is on my radar."

"It should be. You do have a grade point average of 3.7 and all. I see you man!"

My grade point average has helped me secure quite a few private scholarships. Plus, I've been accepted by all the colleges I submitted applications to this year. Hard work pays off.

Then Jessica says, "I'm about to go now. Don't be a stranger. Call me more often. I really want us to stay in touch with each other."

"Most definitely," I say. "Maybe we can pick up where we left off a while back. We should go out on a date and hang out soon."

"I'm cool with that," she says. "See you later."

Jessica walks away strutting like a famous supermodel. Everything about her is simply stunning. I swear that every time she walks away, I can't help but to stare. That's normally the case for everyone else who's around too when she walks away.

Out of nowhere, I feel something tugging on my clothes. I turn around and its Cameron.

"Are you alright Avery?" Cameron asks.

"I'm good little man," I say.

"When you're done drooling over Jessica, can we go get something to eat dude?"

"I was not drooling," I say.

"If you say so," he says. "But your mouth was wide open."

"When you get a little older, you'll understand little man."

"Whatever," he says. "Can we go now?"

"Sure. Let's bounce!"

Chapter Twenty-One

AFTER ANOTHER HOT and interesting summer, today is the day I finally head off to college. Today marks another historical day in my life I'll never forget. I've decided to commit to Fisk University, a small HBCU here in Tennessee. I didn't want to go away too far from my family. I'll only be three hours away from them. I'm really going to miss them while I'm away at school. I'll be looking forward to spending time with them on all my breaks and the holidays. Pastor Wright has volunteered to drive me to school for Mama. For the most part, Pastor Wright has been a major blessing for me and my family. I can always depend on him in a time of need.

Right when I'm about to walk out of the front door, Mama starts crying.

"What's wrong Mama?" I ask.

"I'm alright son," she says, wiping her face. "I'm just going to miss you while you're gone. This will surely be the longest time that we've ever been apart from each other."

"I'm going to miss you too Mama," I say.

"Things won't be the same around here with you gone," she says.

"I know Mama," I say. "I'm sure Cameron will still keep you occupied and busy while I'm gone."

"He definitely will," she says. "I don't want you playing around with school. I want you to stay focused and do your best."

"I will Mama," I say. "You can count on me to take care of business. I promise I won't let you down."

"Okay son. If you ever need anything, make sure you call me and let me know."

"I will. I should be good on cash for the most part. I'll probably do work-study or find a little part-time job to make some money."

"That sounds good. If you decide to do that, just make sure that getting your schoolwork done comes first."

"I will."

"I'm so proud of the young man you've become Avery."

"You've played a big role in that Mama. I've learned so much from you growing up. You've made so many sacrifices and have done so much for me. I'm truly thankful for that."

"I love you son."

"I love you too Mama."

We both embrace each other with a long warm hug. I walk over to Cameron and give him a big hug as well.

"Take care of Mama for me while I'm gone little man," I say.

"No problem bro," Cameron says. "She knows I'm the real man of the house anyway."

I laugh. "I'm sure she does. Hold down the house little man."

"I will. I'll see you soon too. Bring back home some good grades smart guy."

"You know I got this!"

I leave out of the house and meet Pastor Wright at his car. We both load up my luggage into his trunk. I wave goodbye to Mama as I'm getting inside the car. I have so much love and respect for that woman. I'm going to make her very proud. After Pastor Wright cranks up the car, he turns the radio down low and leans back into his seat. I sense another serious conversation that's about to transpire.

"Are you good son?" Pastor Wright asks.

"I'm alright," I say. "But I'm a little worried about my mama."

"Why are you worried?" he asks.

"I just hope she's able to maintain while I'm gone," I say. "Everything is still going good for her at the supermarket, but she's no longer working that other part-time job. It just played out a little while ago."

"Don't worry about your mother son. She's going to be just fine. I'll be checking on your family often to make sure they're good."

"I really appreciate that. Also, I appreciate you taking me off to school today. You're a great man."

"I'll do almost anything for my good people. You know how I get down son."

"I sure do. I'm blessed to have you in my corner."

Without Pastor Wright in my life, I don't know what I'd do. This man has been like a true father figure to me for the longest.

Then Pastor Wright says, "I want you to take care of your business at school son. I don't want you messing around with this."

"That's on my agenda," I say. "I'll be on top of everything at all times. You definitely don't have to worry about that."

"Good," he says. "I want you to pray every day and stay out of trouble. I already had to get you out of one jam while you were here. You're going to be on your own now and I need you to make wise decisions on a regular basis."

"Okay," I say. "But what jam are you talking about Pastor? You lost me on that one."

He smiles at me and says, "I was referring to that time when you were about to try and take out Pistol P from the top of that abandoned building."

My mouth drops. I'm speechless. Did he really just say that to me?

"No . . . way," I say. "How do you even know about that?"

"I told you a long time ago that I know about everything that goes on in my neighborhood," he says. "One thing I've never told you is that I work closely with the city's police department to help them bring down crime in this crazy neighborhood."

"Are you serious?"

"Yeah—I am. I've been working with them for many years now. They have me on payroll. I'm heavily involved in the research process of several open criminal investigations for this neighborhood. I played a huge role in that big bust on BCM."

"Wow."

"That's why I called you that day when you were on the roof of that building."

"It was kind of odd when you were calling me right at that moment."

"When the police and I were preparing to bust BCM, we saw you going up to the roof of that building with that big case. I knew you were about to do something stupid. Then, one of the police officers that was on top of another nearby building saw you take that rifle out of the case. The officer informed us over the radio about what you were doing on the roof and I convinced the police chief to let me handle you."

"That's crazy."

"You nearly messed up the entire bust," he says. "That operation had been planned for many weeks. I couldn't let you mess that up and I had to save you from yourself too."

"Good looking out Pastor," I say. "My mind was completely gone at that point. I just had so many mixed emotions when I decided to do that."

"I know son," he says. "I'm just glad you listened to me and stood down that day. Your life would've completely turned for the worse if you had pulled that trigger."

"I'm glad I didn't pull it either. I would've definitely been behind bars."

"The police still wanted to pursue you afterwards for having that gun and almost messing up the bust, but I convinced them to let it go since everything turned out alright in the end."

"You're a lifesaver. Thank you."

"You're welcome son. The police took that rifle out of the dumpster you threw it in. I want you to *never* illegally possess a weapon like that again."

"I won't. I promise."

"Good. I don't want this conversation we're having right now to ever be brought up with anyone else. I don't want anyone else to know about what I got going on with the police."

"My lips are sealed. That's a brave thing you're doing with the police. I really admire that."

"Thanks son. Changing a neighborhood starts with the people in the neighborhood being a part of the process."

"You're right."

"Trying to change this neighborhood is a difficult task, but I'll continue to do what I'm doing and preach the gospel until it's time for me to retire."

"I hear you," I say. "It's a good chance that things will never change around here."

"That may turn out to be true son, but you never know what can happen. It's worth the shot."

"Yeah—it is. Have you heard anything about the police having any leads on catching the guys that killed Derek?"

"Unfortunately, no. If I hear anything, I'll be sure to let you know. We'll get them son. Don't worry."

"Okay. Thanks Pastor."

"No problem. Put on your seatbelt. Let's get you to school."

It's a real blessing that I managed to survive this neighborhood. Everybody doesn't make it out, especially after getting involved in drugs and the streets. Everybody doesn't get a chance to get out of the ghetto and go to college. That's extremely rare around here. I hardly ever see it happen. I've learned my lesson from all the bad decisions I've made so far. I thank God for this opportunity to better myself. I'm going to work extremely hard so I can get my mama and little brother out of the ghetto. They deserve so much better. I'm sure Derek would be proud of me right now. He'll forever live in my heart and thoughts. Off to college I go. I survived.

Message from the Author

Although this story is pure fiction, it provides an example of the true reality that many young African American males have to endure in their lifetime. In most poverty-stricken African American neighborhoods (the ghetto), drugs and gang presence are considered the norm. When these two elements exist, it's only a matter of time until young males who live in those neighborhoods become actively involved in them. When they get involved in selling drugs and joining gangs, the end result is usually not a favorable outcome for them. Some of these young males turn to selling drugs and joining gangs because of peer pressure, but most of them get involved in these actions because they view them as available options that could help them survive their environment.

To add to the existing circumstances, many of these young males grow up without their biological father being active in their lives. This leaves their mothers to raise and take care of them alone, which is a very daunting task. We continue to see this take place on a regular basis in our society. The lack of a male in the household takes away the potential positive guidance and leadership that a young male desperately needs while growing up. Positive guidance and leadership can help an individual develop good character. Some mothers manage to do a phenomenal job of raising their male offspring on their own, but nothing can completely replace the impact that a father can have on their own son. Oftentimes, some young males who grow up without their biological father in their lives end up having resentment toward them, especially if the father had opportunities to be present and chose not to do so.

All young African American males will have a better chance to succeed in life when we as a nation begin to set them up for success. From a moral standpoint, it's the right thing to do. Setting them up for success will have to come by the hands of all parents, citizens in the community, and our appointed leaders in America. Taking a united approach is the only way our nation will be able to put young African American males in a better position to succeed in life. Taking a united approach is bound to produce positive results and reverse what we've seen take place in our society for far too long. It's time for a change of action. We must create a better culture for all young African American males. They deserve better.

We desperately need African American males to be more active in the lives of their male offspring and to act as positive role models. All fathers should step up to the plate and do what needs to be done. We need all our communities to collectively set the tone for what is tolerable within our neighborhoods. We must work hard to suppress the presence of drugs and gang activity, especially in African American communities that have greatly suffered from these elements. If we don't take an aggressive approach now, more young African American males will continue to get involved in drugs or gangs and will eventually lose their lives in the process. Let's change the current narrative on what the norm typically looks like for the life of a young African American male. This can be done when everyone in society plays their part. Let's save their lives. Their lives matter.

In all, I really enjoyed creating this story to share with others. It took me a great amount of time and effort to write this entire story. After all my hard work, I'm extremely pleased with the outcome. When creating this story, one of my main objectives was to really bring the characters to life with their own unique personalities, personal perspectives, and reactions to certain situations. Furthermore, I wanted to design the characters to behave and react to certain situations like many people would who live in poverty-stricken neighborhoods. Just like Avery, there are many extremely smart adolescents who live in poor and dangerous neighborhoods, looking for a possible way out and a better life. When push comes to shove and life stressors become too overwhelming, getting involved in dangerous acts to make money usually comes into play for some people.

Like Avery's mother Sophia, many African American mothers spend most of their days stressed out and worried because they're unsure if they'll be able to keep their family from becoming homeless and starving. Throughout this story, I aimed to demonstrate Sophia's emotional battle and struggle with her stressful circumstances. Although her circumstances were tough, she continued to do the best she could like most mothers in her shoes would do. Even if it took working multiple jobs to make ends meet, she was willing to do it. While growing up as a child, seeing African American mothers work two jobs was a normal thing in my eyes. It was the only way that most mothers could take care of their family when they didn't have any help. In today's society, that's still the norm for many African American mothers.

I hope *The Struggle: Striving to Survive* has somehow broaden your perspective on what goes on in many poverty-stricken neighborhoods in America. Maybe you can relate to this story from your own personal experiences or things you've witnessed in life. The struggle is definitely real for many people. There are so many families in America who are barely making it and are on the brink of becoming homeless. If you're currently in a good place financially and have a comfortable place to live, be thankful. Also, I hope that you found this story to be very entertaining. I did my best to make this story enjoyable and easy to read. There are so many more different aspects of this book that can be discussed. It was my intention to create a story that provided much room for discussion and made people think. I appreciate each and every one of you for taking interest in this book. Feel free to encourage other people to read this awesome story.

Sincerely,
Johnny Franklin Jr.

About the Author

Johnny Franklin Jr. is a prolific author from Memphis, TN. *The Struggle: Striving to Survive* is his first fiction novel. Besides writing and working on projects, he enjoys spending time with his family and vacationing when possible.

Made in the USA
Las Vegas, NV
23 August 2021